Slashed Potatoes and Grave-y

HONEYPIE MYSTERIES

JOANN KEDER

Edited by: The Editing Fairy

Cover Art By: Molly Burton, Cozy Cover Designs

Paperback ISBN: 978-1-953270-33-7

For Andy
Thank you for giving my life the one thing I didn't realize it needed.

"Every adversity, every failure, every heartache carries with it the seed of an equal or greater benefit."
– NAPOLEON HILL"

Characters

Honeypie Chiffon Sweetwater: inherits her grand-mother's restaurant
Dexter Jenkins: her fourteen-year-old son who hates everything
Tildie Bunce: Dexter's best friend
Eliot Jenkins: Dexter's elusive father, with twins, a new wife and no room for his son
Lem Thornwood: Gram Gram's mysterious boyfriend
Maddysin (Bliss) Noseinair: Honeypie's high school rival
Edna Snarlwood: Gram Gram's loyal employee of thirty years
Basil Thymeson: chef at the diner
Cherrie Crumbleton: owner of the rival pie shop
Gwen Folds: coroner, and owner of The Final Press Cleaners
Bash Sweetwater: Honeypie's Uncle

Chapter One

"Ma'am?"

Honeypie Sweetwater stared out the window of her condo. The rain was coming down in sheets, which was fitting for her current financial situation. Unwillingly, she turned her head to face the stern woman sitting across the table from her.

"I'm sorry, Mrs. Steam, I—"

"It's SIStine, like the chapel? And I'm Ms." She twitched her nose just like the old television show with the witch. *Also fitting.*

"This is your copy of the documents for the foreclosure on this property."

"It's my *home*. We're not talking about a lemonade stand. I raised my son here and started a business—"

"And that failed too, didn't it?"

Honeypie dug what was left of her fingernails into her palms, doing her level best not to lose her cool. "You just look at the numbers. You don't have any idea

1

what my life has been like, or what it took just to put food on the table for my kid some months."

After a brief stare-down that Honeypie felt confident she'd won, the banker leaned back, causing the wobbly wooden chair to creak in protest. She flopped an arm over the back of the chair and stuck her tongue in her cheek before delivering the next blow.

"There is also the matter of your inheritance. The land and property in Washington State will also become our holdings after you sign the paperwork." She shuffled through her papers containing a collection of colorful stickers. "I hear great things about the museum in Misty Cove."

"The Chewseum? I didn't realize that was still open. It's a food museum. Kinda cheesy, get it?"

Ms. Sistine ignored H.P.'s attempt at humor and shoved the documents in front of her. "Please sign on the lines I've highlighted."

Clearly, she didn't understand friendly conversation either.

H.P. grinned. "I don't have a pen." It was a momentary reprieve before the family train wreck went to the gallows.

"What?"

It was Honeypie's turn to lean forward. "I said, I DON'T HAVE A PEN!"

Two could play at this game. She should have felt silly for playing it, but her current status was that of an unemployed sous chef with nothing but a 2001 sedan with expired plates and Dexter's braces. Thank goodness she'd paid *those* off when she received her one and only bonus check at Flour That!

"That's ridiculous! *Every* home has a pen."

"You told me I had to be out by today. Everything I own is packed into my car. The alleged pen, if it ever existed, is buried under several pounds of cookware and Legos."

Ms. Sistine, apparently immune to humor, stood and shoved her chair backward, causing it to hit the wall and splinter into pieces.

"That was a family heirloom!"

It wasn't, but it was a nice way to stick it to the woman who was about to take her last shred of dignity. Luckily, Grandma Honeypie (her namesake), or Gram Gram, as she was affectionately known, left a fully furnished house. She and Dex would crash there for a few days until H.P. could figure out where to go next.

"I'm sorry." Ms. Sistine looked up from her purse, where she'd found numerous tubes of expensive lipstick and set them on the table, probably another slight. It was wasted on Honeypie though. She was a natural beauty who only wore lipstick she found at the gas station.

"I'm going to drive to the nearest quickie mart and get one. This has never happened before!"

Was she expecting sympathy? When she was ready to kick a struggling mom and her teen son out of their home?

"Is there one that's... safe?"

Honeypie suppressed a giggle. She'd worked hard

to get into this neighborhood so that Dexter could go to a good school. Public school, but still a good one.

"You'll have to take your chances, I guess."

Honeypie listened until the harsh clacking of the banker's heels dissipated. She looked at her watch. 4:30. Dex should have been home by now. He was saying goodbye to all his buddies and promised he'd be back in an hour.

The accountant had called after Gram Gram's funeral, giving her a perfunctory, "Your grandmother left her diner to you."

H.P. took one last pass through their condo, thinking of all the memories, both good and bad: her culinary degree, Dex's birth, the disappearance of Dex's father, her meaningful conversations with Gram Gram... all of her life was contained within these walls.

Honeypie leaned her head against the wall in what was once her living room. She remembered when Dex was eight and she told him he could decide the color they painted the living room. He chose fluorescent green.

"Have fun with that, Mrs. Steam."

She leaned her entire body against it, trying to absorb all that she could from her last moments in the first home she'd ever owned. A shimmer of glass caught her eye, and she glanced over at the open hall closet, where a framed photo sat.

Shards of glass covered the floor, but by this point, what did it matter? Picking it up, she realized this was the picture she'd given Dex for Christmas. It was of the

two of them on their one-and-only trip to Misty Cove.
She smiled at her image, her chestnut brown hair
parted to the left and cut at an angle that covered one
grey eye. Honeypie was wearing a light pink lipstick
that day and grinned as she hugged the only two
people in the world she cared about—her Gram Gram
and Dex.

"You don't look forty-two. Is that your brother?"

She'd heard that at least once and enjoyed the
discomfort it brought her son, especially when he was
irritating her. "I look too young to be your mom,
kiddo."

The framed photo sat under his bed for a year and
when she asked him to pack it, this is where it
ended up.

Gram Gram, or Honeypie Lucinda Sweetwater as
others knew her, was an eighty-year-old woman with a
spirit as vivacious as someone half her age. With a silver
mane of hair neatly tied in a bun and the same grey
eyes as her granddaughter, men still clamored to
date her.

She was grinning from ear-to-ear in the picture,
probably thinking of her best off-color joke to tell
them. Honeypie's heart skipped a beat. Oh, how she
missed their talks.

"Go. Now. You have to solve my murder."

Honeypie jumped back. "What?" When no one
answered, she decided it was a side effect of no sleep
and dehydration. "Crying all the tears you can will do
that to ya, Sweetwater."

The sound of—was it moving furniture?—above her head startled her. Nothing remained in their home, except for the table and chairs. Cautiously, she climbed the stairs. It wouldn't be farfetched to think that Dex was playing a trick on her. He tended to do that when he was angry with her.

The noise became louder until she reached Dex's door and now she was certain it was some trick of his. "If you'd spend as much time on schoolwork as you do on scaring the bejeebies out of me, we'd both be happier!"

Taking a deep breath, Honeypie turned the knob and threw the door open in one motion. The room was empty. She was relieved, but also, maybe a little disappointed? This was a connection they shared in an odd sort of way.

She turned to walk back down the stairs and bumped into something. Not exactly a "thing," though.

"Gram Gram?" Honeypie rubbed her hazel eyes. "I guess it's a good thing I'm unemployed. I'll have plenty of time to catch up on my sleep once we get to Washington."

"Sakes, gal. It took a lot of effort on my part to be here. The least you can do is respect that your old grannie is a ghost and not a figment of your imagination."

It wasn't so much that she didn't believe in ghosts, but she didn't believe they were something she'd see in her lifetime.

"Okay, if Dex is playing games, this needs to stop!" She directed her voice down the stairs, just in case he was having a good time somewhere she couldn't see him. It wouldn't be a stretch to think of him disguising his voice from a hiding place. His friends had all the latest in electronics that he could easily borrow.

"We don't have time for this nonsense, Hun Bun."

That was the term of endearment Gram Gram used for her. None of the other twenty-one grandchildren got a nickname and Gram would thump their heads if they tried. "You got this name for a reason, child. Let's make sure we use it."

But when it came to her namesake, things were different. For starters, H.P. was the only grandchild who'd grown up without a mother. The story was that her mother ran off with the only doctor in town when her only child was barely out of diapers. For years, people in Misty Cove blamed her family for their loss of medical care.

The other reason for her special treatment, at least early on, was the fact that she looked nothing like the rest of the Sweetwater grandkids. They were fair-haired and freckle-faced smilers, while Honeypie Chiffon, H.P., had thick, brunette hair and a darkness about her that kept everyone away from her—children and adults alike.

When H.P.'s father also left her, she moved in with Gram Gram, which suited her just fine.

"I'll entertain the idea that you're real. Spit it out."

"You need to get on outta here now. I want you in

that car lickety blitz, before Miss Crankypants returns. Got my buddy, Abdul running interference at the Ten and Twelve Market, but he can only throw things off the shelves for so long."

"It's split, and we're leaving, Gram Gram. What's the rush? Dex isn't even back from his friend's place yet."

"I can't explain it all now, but you can't let my restaurant go back to the bank. If you drive all night, you'll give yourself a few days. That should be long enough."

"Long enough for what?"

The ghost clucked her tongue in a very un-ghost-like way. "Land, child. To solve my murder!"

Chapter Two

H.P. found a twenty-dollar bill in a coat pocket that morning. Honeypie Chiffon Sweetwater took that as a sign that it was time to come clean with her son. This surprise money would buy her a dozen raised glazed peace offerings to soften the blow.

"Nosedive" was the term she'd used when explaining to Dex that they'd have to leave California. A skinny kid, Dexter Jenkins had his mother's thick, wavy hair, except his was chestnut in color, his father's deep blue eyes and a smirk that was all his own.

Dex sat hunched at the table in his vintage t-shirt with his dark curls drooping over his eyes. It was hard to tell whether he was mid-morning or mid-evening because of his perpetual state of wrinkle.

"So, like I was saying, we're going to move to Washington State. I found a bunch of skateboard parks." Honey shoved a rumpled paper in front of him. She had to give her electric can opener to their upstairs neighbor in exchange for two printed pages, which didn't seem like a fair trade.

"Those are in Seattle." He shoved the papers back towards her and slouched against the back of his chair, folding his thin arms across his abdomen. "NOT in Misty Cove."

H.P. bent down and kissed the top of his head, drinking in what was left of his little boy smell.

Ever since fourth grade, when his best friend went through a growth spurt, Dex smelled like a combination of Axe body spray and his lunchbox when he'd forgotten it in his backpack during spring break. Definitely rancid, but with sweet undertones.

"Don't!" He shoved her hand away.

"Look, bud. I know you're upset, but you never know what's waiting for you up there. You like adventure, right?"

Dex stood abruptly, allowing large chunks of donuts to fall onto the floor. "I wish I could live with Dad! At least Florida isn't stupid."

Dex wanted to move in with his father and his new wife in Florida, but they'd just had twins and "didn't have the energy for him." The poor kid cried himself to sleep for almost a month and refused to talk to his dad on the phone ever since.

Honey cocked her head to one side, allowing her hair to flop in front of her eyes. "He did you dirty there. Lots of blended families have more than one kid."

She held her arms open wide and stared. Hard. "You know I'll do this all night if I have to."

Secretly, she feared one day her son would call her bluff, and then she'd be stuck, waiting endlessly for his show of affection. That wasn't today, though. With heavy feet, Dex surrendered to her motherly love.

She drew him in close, her heart attempting to leap out of her chest with each new breath. "How about I make you a deal? We'll give it a month, and if you're absolutely freakin' miserable, we'll come back to San Fran."

There was no possible way for them to come home. None. Honeypie Sweetwater skillfully burned every bridge she'd ever crossed; some on purpose, some just due to the nature of things. No one would hire her again. But she also knew her son needed a lifeline, and she was throwing one in his direction.

"Okay. I guess."

That day, when she drove her car over the curb, narrowly missing a fire hydrant and a butterscotch-colored stray dog, her son displayed shock and then irritation.

"Get in! We're leaving now!"

Luckily, the combination of her surprised appearance and the unusual abruptness in her voice caught him off guard. He got into the car without an argument and San Francisco was in their rearview mirror by the time he spoke.

"I thought we were leaving tomorrow? A kid in my class wanted to say goodbye."

"It's better to get going than to sit in those emotions, don't you think?"

She kept her eyes trained on the road, hoping he didn't ask anything more. He didn't.

As they reached the California/Oregon border, Honeypie glanced over at her sweet boy. His head rested against the window, and he was softly snoring. As much as he tried to avoid it, Dexter was still her baby.

They'd been driving for nine hours with a brief stop for gas. On the way out of town, she'd stopped at a pawn shop, leaving Gram Gram's emerald necklace and her wedding ring to pay for their trip. She paused before handing over the necklace, but didn't need any extra consideration before handing over her wedding ring.

As her car sped down the glistening blacktop, her mind wandered. Though her grandmother must've been heartbroken that her older son disappeared, she never mentioned it around her granddaughter. Her other son, Sebastian, did his best to fill in.

That's because I love you more than all of my other grandchildren.

"Mom! Lookout!"

Her eyes darted back to the road just in time to prevent a collision with a refrigerated milk truck. "Sorry, Dex. Mom's got a lot on her mind."

She reached over and patted his leg, a gesture met with a low grumble of protest. "What do you say we stop for the night? I don't know about you, but I'm starving!"

"I thought we were broke! Isn't that why you dragged me away from my friends so fast?" It was unusual for his brain to overpower his stomach. "Don't try and pull one on me, Mom. I notice things."

The hurt in his voice was almost too much to take. "Yeah, it was, bud. But I sold some of Gram's jewelry on the way out of town, while you were texting your girlfriend. I notice things too."

When he didn't respond, she continued, "A burger and a hot shower tonight will fix everything. Tomorrow, we'll head out nice and early, and—"

"How early?"

Honeypie did the math in her head. "Seven." Alarms were a delicate balance; too early and the boy would pretend he was a corpse, let him get up on his own and the day was half over. "And then we'll drive the rest of the way to Misty Cove. It'll be fun to spend a few months there, right?"

As it seldom did, the false cheeriness in her voice didn't fool Dex. "Dad's not going to find us. What if he changes his mind? What if he wants me?"

Memories of their last face-to-face meeting flashed through her mind. Eliot looked older, somehow more rugged, even though he was living a pampered life of backyard pools and golf Fridays in Florida. The light that used to dance in his brown eyes was gone. "I'm giving you a gift, H.P. You get primary custody of the boy for now. Until you muck it up, like you always do."

"I'll tell you what. When we get settled in Misty Cove, you can give your dad a call. Give him our new address and everything."

Dex shrugged without comment, choosing instead to continue the game on his phone.

After they'd eaten their fill at Burger Oasis and had their showers, she kissed Dex goodnight and closed her eyes.

She smelled the scent of her grandmother, a combination of her signature honey pie and crispy French fries. Though it was a lovely memory, Honeypie wanted to sleep. She rolled over, refusing to allow the image of her grandmother's sweet smile to enter her dreams.

"You know I was murdered, don't you? That's why I helped you escape. Otherwise, I'd tell you to handle your problems first. Running away isn't how we Sweetwaters operate."

Honeypie shot straight up and took a quick optical glance around the room, her room. She looked at the funny ears alarm clock that woke her—or didn't — all through high school. It was three a.m. Dex had fallen asleep on top of the covers with his phone still sitting in his hand. Reaching over from her twin bed to his, she carefully removed the phone before getting up for a drink of water.

Chapter Three

She'd forgotten how nasty the tap water was, like something she scraped off her shoe. Her cousins called it "snot water," and when one of the little ones got out of line, they'd force them to drink an entire glassful. It was even worse punishment than a month-long, no-television grounding doled out by Gram Gram.

Once a week, Gram Gram took the largest stockpot in the restaurant down from the overhead hook and filled it full of tap water. She boiled lemons, limes, or whatever she had on hand. The end result brought diners from three counties. All to drink water.

Honeypie smirked at the memory. "I sure didn't get the marketing gene." She wiped her chin with her arm, finding comfort in yet again another childhood memory.

Grandma Honey's house looked like it had been hermetically sealed. The yellow and brown blobs posing as flowers on the wallpaper and the green shag carpet were pristine.

When they'd arrived the night before, she didn't take the time to remind Dex that they were in hiding. He'd been through enough already.

"I'm gonna call Dad," he said, before slamming the door to Honeypie's old bedroom, causing her boy band posters to wave in protest.

"Sure, hope he answers this time," she replied under her breath.

Though they had some money, there certainly wasn't enough to make a big grocery haul. The letter from her grandmother's lawyer, Lem Thornwood, promised Gram Gram's home would be ready for their arrival. It wouldn't feel right, staying there without Gram Gram, but what choice did she have?

When H.P. went out to the car to retrieve another load of things, she felt something furry around her ankles. Unfortunately, she'd had too much experience with rats in the kitchens of the more questionable restaurants. She was ready to give it a good sound kick, both to relieve the pent-up frustration of driving for two days with a surly teen in the back and to release the irritation that came along with her crazy delusions. When she looked down and realized it wasn't, in fact, a rat at all. It was a black-and-white cat, still a kitten.

"Well, aren't you a cutie?" She bent down and ran her hand down its soft back as the cat arched up to meet her. The cat was purring so loud its little body was shaking.

"I'm sorry we won't be here long enough to get to know you, little guy."

The cat emitted a squeaky sound, not so much a "meow," but closer to a "weep!" in protest.

"Okay, okay. I'm sure we can find something for you to eat. Just give me a minute."

She pulled Dex's camo-green suitcase out of the back seat. "Follow me, little one!"

The kitten was gone. It would have been nice to have a pet. She and Gram Gram had a cat named Muffin for six years. When Uncle Sebastian moved in, he insisted they re-home her because of his allergies. It was one of the most painful memories she had, the day they handed Muffin over to her school rival.

When she got inside and shut the door, she tripped over the entryway rug and the suitcase, and the rest of her belongings went flying. Luckily, it was just her ego that got bruised.

Tears of frustration welled up in her eyes as she lay on the rust-colored rug, one purchased during her childhood. "What am I doing? The bank will figure out soon enough where I am! This is insanity!"

She felt something on her back and in a minute, the sound of a miniature freight train filled her ears.

"How did you get in here? And aren't you a persistent little thing? Go on home now!"

The kitten displayed no signs of moving; instead, he stretched out on H.P.'s back as though he planned a long nap.

"Dex? Honey, could you..." It was a fruitless effort, expecting him to come when she called. "Forget it."

Luckily, her phone remained in her jeans pocket. She pulled it out and typed, "Need you for a sec, please!" It was iffy whether he would respond when he was in a mood like this.

After several minutes, during which time she found herself relaxing to the point of feeling drowsy, she heard the bedroom door open. "What?" he snapped.

"Just one minute of your time, I promise."

Dex's socks made a thumping sound on the floor as he walked to the entryway. One of the marvels of teendom that H.P. couldn't figure out—how did that kid make so much noise with socks?

She smelled his feet before she saw his body, but now wasn't the time for *that* conversation. "Dex, honey, could you please GENTLY take this kitty off my back and find something in the kitchen for him to eat?"

His theatrical sigh was a cross between a deflating hot-air balloon and a walrus who missed lunch. "Why did you lie on the floor in the first place? Don't you know that cats like to sit on you?"

"The cat found me after—never mind. Just take the cat and I'll finish unloading the car. Unless you'd rather help me with the suitcases?"

Instantly, she felt his hand reach down and scoop up the kitten. The little guy made a slight squeak in protest before returning to his purring.

Turning around to get back in bed, she bumped into her grandmother. Instinctively, Honeypie opened her mouth to scream, but nothing came out.

"Sorry, dear. I can't have you waking the boy. He needs his rest, don't you think?"

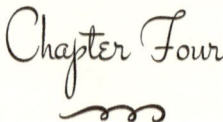

Chapter Four

"It's been real cool talking to you again, Gram Gram. And I appreciate your giving me the heads up to get out of town. But you aren't real. I'm hallucinating and if this doesn't end soon, Dex won't wait for his father's invitation. He'll be on the next bus to Florida."

Gram Gram smacked her lips like she always did when she found something distasteful. H.P. felt the same shame as she did when she set a fire in the girls' locker room. There were copious amounts of smacking that day.

"Child, your worst fault is this attitude. You've never been able to accept things at face value. It's called entertrust."

"Right," Honeypie conceded. Boy, her mind was doing a number on her. She was even including her grandmother's made-up words. "I believe the word you're looking for is 'entrust,' and that's a whole different..." She paused, realizing the absurdity of arguing with herself. "Okay. Let's say, for a reason I can't fathom at the moment, that you were murdered and didn't die from a freak scissor accident. What proof do you have? And I'm not saying I believe this is anything more than a bad dream."

"There's a few folks in Misty Cove who were a little too pleased by my passing. People who tried to take my diner away from me."

H.P. grinned. "Oh, like the Christmas story! I never liked that."

"No, not like the Christmas story." Gram Gram's disgust was evident. "Like people who wanted me dead."

Instantly, the expression on H.P.'s face changed. "Who was it? And why didn't the police investigate?"

"Guess you've forgotten all about the police department in Misty Cove. As long as the serial killer doesn't leave a mess on their doorstep, they don't bother."

She had, in fact, forgotten the unspoken rules of small-town living. Calling the police was something done only when teens vandalized school property.

"Now, pull out your whoop-see-doodle and take this down."

"My phone? That's a weird thing to use in a dream."

Gram Gram's dream ghost gave H.P. the living Gram Gram's famous, "Don't cross me!" look.

"You know, Dex and I are headed to Canada. We might not have time to check them all out, especially if you've got a bunch of people who wanted you dead."

The thought was ludicrous. Everyone in town adored her grandmother, the woman who raised her five children on her own and then several grandchildren, including H.P. But it was a dream and anything was possible. "Okay, I'm ready. Tell me the names of alllll the people who wanted you dead, Gram Gram."

"You're making fun of me now, child. You know what I used to say about that."

"It's all fun and games until somebody touches the burner," H.P. repeated with a dramatic roll of her eyes. "Which doesn't pertain at all to what we're talking about, Gram Gram."

"Well, we'll see about that. I left my diner to you for a reason, Honey Buns. For now, you'll need their names. Get your what's-a-giggle out of your pocket and write this down."

Her grandmother's language was only understood by family, which now made perfect sense. H.P. was missing her grandmother and all the good memories they'd made together. She'd barely shed a tear when Uncle Bash called to tell her Gram Gram died. Releasing it through a dream was much safer and less likely to affect Dex. "Go for it."

Gram Gram's ghost laughed softly. For the first time, H.P. really studied her. If this series of dreams ended soon, she'd at least have these memories of a stunning ghost who brought forth the best in the person who raised her.

Gram's face, though faintly translucent, retained the gentle, loving expressions that characterized her in life. Her eyes, a soft, misty hue, seemed to hold depths of wisdom and untold stories. A comforting smile played on her lips, too.

Her hair was silvery-white, reminiscent of the last time H.P. saw her. It flowed around her like a halo of moonlight, with soft curls that drifted ethereally as if stirred by an unseen breeze instead of being pulled back in a tight bun, her usual look.

Gram Gram's attire was a nod to H.P.'s own eclectic style. She appeared in a long, flowing dress that seemed to be made of a shimmery material in different shades of pastel blues, pinks, and lavenders, changing subtly as she moved.

Gram Gram never dressed so fancy. On the few days off she'd taken, she insisted on wearing her "housecoat."

"It's a robe, Gram Gram," H.P. protested, hoping that label would force her grandmother to change before friends stopped by. "You only wear that when you're alone."

"Who says? I'll do what I want in my own home. Thank you kindly."

To finish her outfit, a Honeypie Diner apron covered her glimmering robe. It, too, changed colors.

"Maddysin Noseinair," Gram Gram said matter-of-factly. "She's the first one you need to check out."

"She's still around? I thought she was going to Paris, or somewhere equally pretentious."

"Oh, she's still around. Still just as nasty as always."

Honeypie thought she detected emotion in Gram Gram's voice. It made her wistful for a terrible time in her life. She'd come home after a day of teasing and taunting and Gram Gram cut a slice of her original honey pie alongside a tall, frothy glass of milk and slid them in front of H.P. without speaking. By the time she'd finished eating, Maddysin was out of her head.

"Maddysin darkened my doorstep at least once a week, telling me about a massage parlor or some such nonsense. I shooed her away just as quickly as she came."

"Hmm. Why would she come just to tell you that?"

Gram Gram made a swishing gesture with one hand. "You'd have to ask her, and that's your first assignment. Are you typing that?"

H.P. glanced at her phone, where she'd typed weird dream, bullet points. "Yep. Got it. What else, Gram?"

"There's a gal who popped in last summer, just as sweet as syrup. Wanted to know about my pies and where my recipes came from. Next thing I know, she's got a shop of her own two blocks over. The nerve! Her name is Cherrie Crumbleton, and she's made no secret about wanting to buy my diner. Still twithers my knickers."

Though she wanted to tell her grandmother that it would have made a lot of sense to sell a successful business and retire to Florida, or somewhere equally sunny, now didn't seem like the appropriate time. "Cherrie Crumbleton, got it. Who's next?"

Gram Gram sighed. "I do hate to bring it up, but my lawyer didn't show up at my funeral. He's a good man, and it breaks my heart to suspect him. We had so many wonderful times together."

H.P. shuddered. "Why would your lawyer come to your funeral in the first place?"

"Mom? Who are you talking to?"

Dex appeared bleary-eyed and still wearing the same clothes he had on before she'd asked him to take a shower.

"Oh, just talking to myself, bud. You know how I am."

He shrugged, uninterested in his mother's where-abouts in the middle of the night, before returning to his room.

"Sleep well, bud! We have a big day tomorrow!"

He mumbled something under his breath that she was certain she didn't want to hear.

When she turned around, Gram Gram was gone.

Chapter Five

The last time she'd seen the diner, it was a drab mixture of turquoise peeling paint and black vinyl booths that were held together by duct tape.

Now, the diner had an upbeat, retro vibe with shiny red vinyl booths, a black countertop, and black-and-white tiles on the floor. Painted tiles decorated the walls, each one painted cheerily with a different type of pie. It was so... unlike Gram Gram. All of H.P.'s child-hood and into her early adult life, the diner never changed.

"Did a bunch of upgrades last year. I told her it was a waste of time. That we were both gonna die before she'd get her money back."

Edna Snarlwood had what H.P. referred to as a "timeless" look. Her grey hair hung limply around her face with a large, brown barrette yanking a section backward tightly, so tightly it must've hurt.

In addition, Edna wore black, large-framed brown

glasses that could very well have framed her face for half a century. Every single part of her body sagged in protest of her frosty personality. A smile never crossed her surly face in the thirty years she'd worked there.

"Edna!"

H.P. reached out instinctively to hug her old acquaintance, forgetting momentarily that Edna wasn't the hugging type.

"Didn't think you'd actually show. Since you missed the funeral and all."

Ouch. Good old Edna always knew right where to stick the knife. The trick was to block it before the wound became too deep. "Yes, you're correct, Edna. I heard it was lovely, though."

"From whom? You don't talk to anyone in your family anymore."

H.P. opened her mouth to disagree, (though it was, unfortunately, accurate) but before she could respond, she saw the silhouette of another person in the kitchen out of the corner of her eye. "Edna, there's someone here!" she hissed.

Edna turned the upper part of her body around. "Oh. That's Basil Thymeson. The chef. We seem to go through about one a year."

"In all the years I worked here, Gram Gram never hired a chef. What changed?"

"A fancy spa and restaurant across town, for starters," Edna remarked without emotion. "I went over there to check out the menu one day. Fifty dollars for a steak. Probably have to buy the silverware, too."

Shadowy no more, a man appeared at the front of the house. The friendly-looking guy wiped his hands on his half-apron before extending one to H.P. Basil reminded her of many of the chefs she'd encountered in San Francisco, combining an air of worldly experience with a touch of the bohemian. In his late forties, he carried an aura of well-seasoned vitality. A tall, thin man, his face was framed by shoulder-length, wavy hair, the color of dark chestnut with streaks of silver starting to show, especially at the temples. He wore a multicolored headband, common for chefs in the city, both to keep their hair out of their eyes and hold back the sweat from a hot kitchen.

His eyes were a deep, thoughtful green and his skin bore the subtle tan of someone who spent considerable time outdoors, in somewhere other than perennially cloudy Misty Cove.

Basil even wore the signature shoes of San Francisco chefs, colorful sneakers with a tread resembling measuring spoons.

"HP., right?" He grinned as he offered a hand in greeting. "I heard you might be showing up as an interim manager until the next owner arrives."

H.P. shot Edna a dirty glance. That sounded exactly like the gossip the old woman would spread. Edna, for her part, stuck to her vacant expression.

"For now, the next owner is me. My son and I needed a break, and—"

"Debts, right? I heard all about it."

She took a free hand and pushed her hair out of

her eyes. "It sounds like your source has a few screws loose. None of that is true."

Edna pivoted and stomped off to the kitchen with both the chef and H.P. watching. "She's a pistol, am I right?" Basil mused.

H.P. nodded. "That's one word for it. What brings you to Misty Cove, Basil?"

"Family, mostly. I grew up in Seattle and I've always wanted to start my own café, but the timing was never right. My sister, who is also in the 'biz,' as we say, thought I should get a little experience under my belt first. Your grandmother very kindly allowed me to revamp the menu to test out my recipes on her regulars." Basil smiled broadly. "I hear you have quite the impressive resumé!"

That bit of information couldn't have come from Edna, given her general lack of interest in anything that didn't involve the diner. "My resumé is lengthy, that's for sure." She glanced down at the bright and cheery menus that showcased a new logo, one featuring a sketch of their signature honey pie.

"Maybe you and I can put our heads together later. Your grandmother took her signature recipes off this new menu. No matter how much her customers complained, she refused to bring them back. Maybe you remember them?"

She hadn't worked in the family diner since high school and only cooked on the rare occasions her Uncle Bash or another relative was sick. "I could try."

"Great!" Basil said enthusiastically. "Can't wait to

prepare her special dishes again and give the community another chance to connect with Honeypie Sweetwater."

The idea wasn't half bad. "I'd better familiarize myself with the menu. Maybe we can chat later?"

"Sure, I'd like that! It's great to have some new blood in Misty Cove, even for a brief time. We've all grieved your grandmother's loss. She was a special woman. Who would have known a pair of scissors would have done her in?"

H.P. shrugged, unsure how to respond.

Basil nodded and disappeared into the kitchen. Searching underneath the counter, she found a black-and-white apron starched and folded. As she slipped it over her head, Honeypie remembered the first time she officially joined the staff. In an informal ceremony with two regulars and one drunk who wandered in off the street, Gram Gram placed an apron over her head and H.P. felt like she'd been crowned queen of the diners.

"Hun Bun, hand me a whoopsie doodle."

It was Gram Gram's catchall term, and all her grandchildren made a great game of figuring out exactly what she meant.

"For today, my granddaughter will be cleaning the menus and making sodas. You folks show her the ropes now."

Vlad, Beatrice and all the other regulars who'd since passed away applauded her newfound title of table clearer. At the ripe old age of ten, she earned her first tip—two dollars from Vlad for bringing him a clean glass. "Don't spend it all in one place," he said with a wink.

As an eleven-year-old, Honeypie didn't think she was smart enough to work in Gram Gram's diner. She's seen how fast the staff had to move, sometimes filling a soda while they wrote out a ticket with the other hand. Gram Gram, sensing her doubts, rubbed her back reassuringly. "You've got it in your blood, Hun Bun."

That Saturday and every Saturday thereafter, H.P. raced to the diner as soon as the sun came up. She didn't care that it was the one day of the week that she wasn't awoken by her pink alarm clock. Being an employee of the family diner meant something.

Her curiosity piqued by the addition of new additions, H.P. pulled a pile of menus out from the same shelf used when she was eleven. Honey *chiffon* pie? Meatloaf with mashed turnips and garden greens?

The old recipes weren't just menu items; they were Gram Gram's identity. Her heart sunk as she wondered what had become of those recipes? Knowing Gram, they were tucked away in a shoebox that no one would find for the next hundred years.

The menu changes and the remodel made it impossible to find the original Honeypie Sweetwater anywhere. The more she thought about it, though, the more she realized, from a business perspective, how wise it was. Restaurants can't continue to thrive without updates.

H.P. hummed to herself as she wiped syrup and

ketchup blotches from the shiny surface. It had been weeks since she felt this relaxed.

"If this invigorates you, come to my restaurant. I've got a whole pile of menus just waiting for your grubby, little hands."

Honeypie jumped, dropping the pile of menus she'd just cleaned on a bottle of ketchup that spilled its contents on several of them. She spun around to find herself face-to-face with her high school nemesis, Maddysin Noseinair.

H.P. noticed, with some amusement, that her honey-colored hair was pulled back so tightly in a ponytail that it made her brows arch like a cartoon villain.

In high school, Maddysin's mother bought her twenty cheerleader uniforms, so she always had a clean one to wear to school. Today, however, she wore a white blouse with three unbuttoned buttons underneath a blue business suit. This Maddysin looked less like a perennial cheerleader and more like she was speaking at the real estate conference.

"I heard you were back in town. Bummer about your grandma."

Honeypie swallowed hard. "What brings you by, Maddisyn? Here for pie? Last I knew, you didn't eat my grandmother's recipes."

"Still don't. I'm sure they all use lard. I've opened my own wildly successful spa and Bliss My Heart—a locally sourced and fabulously successful restaurant.

And it's Bliss now. I go by my middle name because it's much easier to spell."

You can say that again.

"I was shocked when I heard she'd left her business to you. I mean, of all the Sweetwaters, you're—"

"The biggest mess? How kind of you."

There was no use hiding the fact that this woman made her want to break every dish in the entire establishment.

"I was going to say the furthest away. But now that I see you, I realize you're right." Maddysin opened a camel-colored wallet and pulled out a light-blue business card with the word "BLISS" written across the top in gold letters. "I'd be happy to set you up for a facial and have someone talk to you about those crow's feet. You don't want to look like you're on death's door if you're going to be the face of Honeypie's Diner."

H.P. dropped her eyes to the menu in front of her, doing her best not to feed into this woman's games. As she did, she noticed something shiny about to fall out of Maddysin's large leather bag.

Catching an expensive bronze letter opener before it hit the floor, H.P. took a moment to examine it before handing it back. Were those specks of blood on the handle?

"Where'd you get that letter opener, Maddysin? It's a weird thing to carry around in your purse, unless—"

Maddysin snatched it from her hands. "Unless what? I'm planning to take out my frustration on an old rival?" Her eyes could have bored a hole through

H.P., had there not been an apron and nametag in the way.

Try a slice of our NEW signature pie, the Maverick Maple Bacon and Pecan with a scoop of our housemade vanilla ice cream on top! You'll be asking for seconds!

When did they start making ice cream? Gram Gram never mentioned it.

"Blissful Relaxation is the ultimate in relaxation. Currently, we own a high-end restaurant, a full-service spa, and a line of detoxifying shakes. The only thing we're missing is a middle-of-the-road greasy spoon for the budget conscious traveler." Bliss's obviously restructured nose wrinkled as if those words smelled bad coming out of her mouth.

Honeypie could feel her ears burning. That was how it always started, before the red blotches made their way down her neck and onto her chest. Her anger wasn't easy to hide.

"Maddysin, Bliss, or whatever you're calling yourself, if my grandmother didn't sell to you, she had a very good reason. I trust her judgment. Now, if you'll slither back to your fancy spa, I've got work to do." H.P. made walking gestures with her fingers to emphasize her point.

The school bully hadn't changed. She was still superficial and evil. Any number of times, H.P. stepped in between Maddysin and the underling she'd chosen to torture that day.

Maddysin crossed her arms and grinned, exhibiting teeth a color of white that had yet to be named.

"I assume you've got children to sacrifice, so you'd better be on your way," H.P. added for emphasis.

H.P. began wiping the surface of the menu she was holding. *If someone up there still likes me, please send an entire bus full of rowdy children right now.*

"I can't wait to watch you fail. And when you do, I'll swoop in and buy this place for a fraction of what I offered your grandmother."

Nope. Not today.

As she walked through the swinging doors to the kitchen, Basil looked up from chopping vegetables.

"Oh, I know that look. You must've run into a school chum. The saying, 'You can't go home again,' is never wrong."

"You're a mind reader, Basil!" It felt good to have someone on her side. "I won't be here long enough to let these people get under my skin, though."

"We're going to get along just fine." Basil smiled widely. "Care to help me chop?"

Chapter Six

Working as a subordinate to huge egos, H.P. had learned to focus on her tasks and nothing else. The fancy kitchens of San Francisco were so specialized, there was someone who came in just to make salads. But here in the diner, everyone chipped in to help.

"Thanks, Gram Gram, for hiring a chef. It's so nice to have another professional in the kitchen!"

She glanced around the diner and was relieved to find herself alone. "You've got to stop talking to yourself, Sweetwater!"

She'd barely had time to think about Maddysin, between assisting Basil and waiting on customers. Luckily, Gram Gram's diner still attracted a big lunch crowd.

Now that customers were waning, her thoughts turned to Maddysin, and boy, were they disturbing. *Did Maddysin kill Gram Gram? How did she get inside the house?*

She was certainly evil enough. And if memory served, the man who spawned the devil owned a knife-sharpening business. This was getting her bordering on insanity. Honeypie Chiffon Sweetwater was trying to solve a crime that was nothing more than a recurring dream.

"Earth to Mom!"

Dex was waving a hand in front of her face, one that smelled like French fries and school supplies.

"Oh! Sorry, hon. I've got a million things on my mind today. How was school?"

The guilt she'd experienced that morning when she stopped in front of Zigg Wobbler Middle School (named after the only famous person to come from Misty Cove, a high school football star who went on to play professionally) returned now as though an alarm had gone off. He refused her offer to come with him. "Just to the office, to make sure they've got all your files, bud," she protested to the back of his head.

Dex turned to get out of the car and stared hard at his mother. "I know the way back to the diner. Don't pick me up. I've got enough problems."

Much to her delight, his 3:30 p.m. mood had improved considerably. "Tell me all about your day, bud! What are your teachers like?"

He flopped down on a red vinyl padded stool and shrugged. "Can we talk about it later? I'm starving."

How could she forget? This boy never had a full mark. "Sure, sure. Tell me what you want. A burger? Grammie started making pizzas too."

The door jingled and they both stared as a caramel-skinned girl with long, wavy hair entered. She sat down next to Dex, flopping two thick textbooks beside her before smiling expectantly at H.P.

"What can I get you, young lady? Do you come here to do your homework every day? Maybe we can start a club!"

"Mom—" Dexter protested.

"Oh, no. I don't need help with my homework." She smiled before glancing beside her. "I'm here to help Dexter. He asked for a history tutor, and I volunteered."

H.P.'s mouth had to have hit the floor hard, but she was so stunned she didn't feel it. "Dex—my son—asked for a tutor?" He was the smartest kid in his class at P.S. 418. They'd asked for her to consider skipping him a grade more than once.

Dexter's face turned the color of cooked beets.

"Oh, you're his mom? You look so young! It's a pleasure to meet you. I'm Matilda Bunce. Tildie for short."

She thrust a long arm across the counter.

Still struggling to process everything taking place, H.P. shook her hand and stared at the girl.

"How did you two meet?"

Out of the corner of her eye, Dex shook his head with vigor, but she didn't care. H.P. knew a little secret. Her son pretended to have many girlfriends to impress his friends. Girls he'd met "from across town." In reality, he was far too shy to have an actual, living, breathing girlfriend, and that suited H.P. just fine.

Tildie glanced at Dex and giggled. "I try to make newcomers feel welcome because I know what it's like to be an outsider." She paused to pull a small, pink coin purse from her backpack. "Plus, you may not have noticed, but my vocabulary is twice that of the average eighth grader. That makes me more of a target than friend material."

"Well, you're just lovely, darling. What would you like to eat? It's on the house, of course."

"Mom, Tildie doesn't eat—" His protests were getting louder.

"I'd love an apple."

H.P. cocked her head to the side, sizing up the pint-sized prowess on display in front of her. "You're something, Miss Tildie. I've been a mom for fourteen years and not once in that time has anyone asked me for something healthy."

"Mom—" Dexter was one step below meltdown now.

She glanced at her son, who was desperately trying to communicate telepathically a message she refused to receive.

"Okay, okay. I get it. I'll go into the kitchen and see if I can scrounge up an apple. We've been making pies all day, but I'm sure there's a piece of untampered-with fruit somewhere."

Though she'd announced her exit, H.P. remained planted in place. The entire experience—Dex having a good day, Dex making a friend, and Dex, the smartest kid she knew, asking for a tutor—was just as hard to process as her earlier meeting with her old high school rival.

"Ms. Sweetwater? Do you happen to have purified water as well? I'm parched!"

"Huh? Sure, hon. You bet."

Dex made a shooing motion with his hand, attempting to persuade her to leave them alone.

"Did someone order a burger with fries and an apple?"

Basil appeared, holding a plate with crisp, brown fries and a juicy burger. In his other hand he held a deep red Gala apple.

Dex's eyes opened wide. "When did Gram Gram hire a fancy chef? And how did you finish that so fast?"

"Right? That was my question too." H.P. was relieved they finally had common ground. "Basil, this is my handsome Dexie and his TUTOR, Tildie."

"I'm not a baby! Use my real name!"

Basil slid the hot plate in front of Dex and bent down, presenting the apple to Tildie as though it were a rare gem.

"Sorry. Basil, this is my son, Dexter."

Basil and Dex exchanged a hand bro handshake, one H.P. always found ridiculous. Only today, it was another connection Dex made.

"Nice to meet you, brother. I'm sure we'll be seeing a lot of each other. Let me know what you think of the burger. I'm great at reading people's hunger. The minute you walked through the door, I knew you were a burger and fries kind of guy."

Dex thrust three fries in his mouth and chewed with enthusiasm. "Yeah! I'll be here every day after school!"

H.P. stared at Basil with wonder. "I'm starting to understand why Gram Gram hired you!"

"I'll be back in a moment with your water, Miss Tildie." Basil disappeared through the swinging doors, bringing another long pause in the conversation.

The only sound was a decisive crunch from Dex devouring the fries. The executive chef at *Fried* told H.P. the sound of a crispy crunch was the sound of money because a good fry brought people back again and again.

"Mom, didn't you say you had something to do in the kitchen?"

Her son's eyes carried the pleading look of a boy who desperately wanted to prove his game, an act that was impossible with his mother watching.

"Oh, that's right." H.P. snapped her fingers and made a show of her revelation.

"I was going to take inventory of the walk-in. Will you excuse me?"

Basil opened his mouth, but instead of protesting, he frowned as she walked by. If he didn't understand the rules of middle school, she wasn't going to be the one to explain them.

Finding a clipboard and some lined paper in the office, she decided a back-up inventory wasn't a bad idea. The walk-in was a giant cooler that held fruits and vegetables, raw meat, dressings, and anything that might spoil. The frozen foods were housed in a walk-in deep freeze on the other side of the room.

She grabbed an old sweater Gram Gram used when she worked in the chilly space and opened the door. What she found shocked her. Gram Gram's normally well-organized cooler was now a disaster. She glanced around at the disorganization. Fruit and vegetable boxes, some half-open, some empty, covered the shelves. In the very back of the cooler, duct tape was crisscrossed around four boxes labeled, "Auntie Jean's Frozen Peas."

An eerie quiet made the cooler seem ominous. Those weird dreams were starting to seep into every part of her life. They had her questioning every waking moment. Even with the dim light overhead, it was dark, and it smelled like... what was that smell? Oh, yeah... Gram Gram's honey pie, cooling on the shelf between the kitchen and dining area.

H.P. closed her eyes and drank in the memory: sitting on the counter, swinging her legs as Gram Gram taught her how to roll out pie crusts. "Always roll the crust away from your body, Hun Bun."

No other grandchild was given the opportunity to join their grandmother after hours at the diner, making H.P. feel special.

The hairs on the back of her neck stood up, and the temperature dropped in the room, leaving her

feeling nauseous. Once they were settled—somewhere
—she'd find a doctor.

"Didn't I tell you that girl was no good?"

H.P. jumped. "Who's there?"

"The same Gram Gram you've convinced yourself
is a dream. You'll be relieved to know that you aren't in
need of one of those shrinky-dink talkers."

"Psychiatrist, Gram Gram."

She blinked. Then blinked again. It was daylight.
She remembered shutting off her alarm, dropping Dex
off at school...

"Can we save time and cut to the part where I'm
appearing in front of you? I have an eternity, but
you're still on the human clock, darling."

"You're telling me that I'm seeing a—"

"Ghost. Yes, my love. And just as I mentioned
before, I need your help with finding my killer."

H.P. swallowed hard. *Pull yourself together, Sweetwater.* "You... mentioned Maddysin, and how her wish
was to buy you out. She came in today and ever since,
I've been mulling it over."

"What's that, Hun Bun? How much of her is still
the original from the factory?"

A giggle escaped her mouth. "Yes—no—whether
she has it in her to kill someone. I can't picture the
woman who wouldn't touch cafeteria pizza because
the cheese might permanently stain her insides would
get her hands dirty with murder."

"Go visit her. See if you can find the murder
weapon while you're at it." Gram Gram floated around

H.P.'s head as though she were a fish swimming in a tank. "You don't believe I fell on scissors, do you? I was still just as light on my feet as I was when your grandfather and I won the county boogie dance off."

H.P. frowned. "Okay. I'll swallow my pride and go to her spa tomorrow."

"Before you do that, stop by the coroner's office. You might find some information there."

"You can talk to yourself just as easily in the office. There're bills needing to be paid."

H.P. jumped at the sound of Edna's stern voice. "Sorry, Edna. I was looking for the... lettuce. I'll be out in a minute."

Once again, when she turned back around, Gram Gram was gone.

Chapter Seven

The Final Fold Dry Cleaners was the second-oldest building in Misty Cove, second only to Maddysin's family home, a block-long monstrosity built by her great-great-grandfather.

H.P. looked at her watch. Ten 'til three. It only took six minutes to walk to the cleaners from the diner, an amusing thought for a woman who gave no thought to walking three miles to her latest job. How did anyone in Misty Cove get any exercise when the entire town was reachable within minutes?

"Take a number!" a disembodied voice growled. The humid room was full of irritated customers, each lined up so close to each other, their arms were touching. The customers, it seemed, had much to discuss with their local dry cleaner.

H.P. stood off to the side to avoid touching people she didn't know. It also gave her a chance to size up the dry cleaner and figure out why Gram Gram was so insistent they meet.

"I hear you, Mrs. Addams. Your aunt DID look unnatural at her funeral. But I don't prepare the bodies. I'm the one they call if the death was suspicious, and your aunt slipped on her homemade butter and hit her head on the table. You'll have to take it up with Rich over at The Final Countdown Mortuary. Tell him you didn't appreciate your sister, the nun, being made up to look like the prostitute from the musical, 'Ilene's House of Ill Repute.'"

The woman turned so sharply that she stepped on the toe of the next person in line, someone who had the misfortune of wearing flip-flops. Both women stormed out in a huff, shortening the line considerably.

When it was finally H.P.'s turn, she shook her head, feeling empathy for this poor soul. "Is this what every day is like here? It must be exhausting!"

Gwen Folds sported a short mushroom hairdo, predominantly silver with streaks of her original ebony hue. A thick, mustard-colored sweater swallowed her small frame and large, tortoise-shell-framed glasses sat low on her nose.

"Oh, honey, you have no idea." Gwen pushed the glasses up her nose. "These people think I'm either their shrink or a magician who can remove six-year-old red wine stains from white linen. Nobody is ever happy with me."

Staring into the poor woman's deep brown eyes,

H.P. felt a twang of guilt. "This was a mistake. Maybe I should come back another day."

As she turned to leave, Gwen grabbed her forearm with surprising force. "Wait! Please don't go." She looked both ways before whispering, "I could use a few minutes with a normal person. I haven't seen you before; are you new in town?"

Normal. Now that was a laugh.

"I lived here as a kid. My son and I moved back when my grandmother died, to run her diner." She smiled before adding, "We're just here temporarily. I'll be selling soon."

Gwen's eyes grew wide. "You're Honeypie Sweetwater's granddaughter? I thought I met all of her family at the funeral."

"I wasn't there. My life is... complicated."

She glanced away, hoping Gwen didn't catch the red blotches quickly spreading down her neck. Explaining her trainwreck of a life was the quickest way to lose a potential friend. She'd seen them come and go many, many times.

"Don't I know it. Maybe we can meet for a drink some day and I'll entertain you with my family stories. What brings you in? Need an eighty-year-old stain removed from antique linen, or do you want to chat about something else?"

"I..." H.P. cleared her throat.

"We skipped right over the intro, didn't we? I'm Gwen Folds, coroner, laundromat owner by inheritance, and gal in need of a good friend."

H.P. could feel her shoulders lowering. "Nice to meet you, Gwen. I'm Honeypie, but most people call me H.P."

They shook hands before H.P. continued. "More than likely, I'll be selling to Maddysin—I mean, Bliss. We can certainly get a drink before then!"

"Oh. Her." Gwen rolled her eyes. "She's been pestering most of the business owners in town to sell to her. It's like she wants to start a cult. A spa cult."

They both chuckled.

"I don't think that's what brought you in, H.P. One of my many talents is my ability to tell when someone's lying."

H.P. ran her fingers around the neck of her uniform while she looked anywhere but straight ahead. "I wanted to ask you about my grandmother's cause of death. I read that it was natural causes, but scissors to the throat doesn't seem natural at all."

"Well, it's kind of a catch-all term. We in the biz use it to explain deaths without suspicion. Between you and me," Gwen leaned her short body over the counter and cupped a hand beside her mouth. "I don't think it was an accident. The angle of the wound wasn't consistent with a fall."

"Why did you put that on her death certificate if you didn't believe it was true?"

Gwen cocked her head to the side. "Surely, I don't need to explain small town politics to you? Unless someone looks like Swiss cheese and we find a gun nearby, it's 'natural causes,' here in Misty Cove."

H.P. nodded, the anger in her welling up. How dare they gloss over the death of a beloved Misty Cove icon! "Who found her? Was it her boyfriend?"

"That's my recollection, but let me check for sure."

She hopped up on a wobbly stool and began typing at a furious pace on a one-size-fits-all computer. Apparently, Gwen didn't attempt to separate the two businesses. "Oh, that's right. It WAS her gentleman friend, Lem Thornwood. They made plans for a drive down the coast, so he stopped to get picnic supplies before heading over to her home." Gwen's little chest heaved before continuing. "Witness says he knocked on the door several times before realizing something was wrong. Witness went around to the side of the house, where he was able to gain entrance through an open window. Witness says..." Gwen glanced up, perhaps realizing this was all more detailed than a relative wanted to hear.

"Keep going. I need to hear this."

"Witness says he found Honeypie Sweetwater lying beside her bed with the scissors stuck—"

"Okay, okay. I know the rest." H.P. couldn't bear thinking about it anymore. This was a woman who should have been given the opportunity to die peacefully in her sleep.

"Was there anything else?"

Gwen's lips moved, but no sound came out.

"Excuse me, I'm in a hurry to get back to the diner. Edna has a dentist appointment soon and she'll walk out whether I'm there or not."

"Yeah, I was just reading that your grandmother was lying on her cellphone. When I got there, I do recall a bloody footprint. I took a photo, but the sheriff said it was Lem's shoe, so I didn't bother putting it in my report. You know he was married, right? They were the gossip of the town."

H.P. bit her lip.

Gwen's face turned ashen as she bonked herself in the side of the head. "Oh, boy. You didn't know. Bad Gwen! Bad Gwen!"

H.P.'s face felt hot, and the room began to spin, just as it did when Eliot told her he was leaving her for a woman he'd met online.

"You look like you're going to pass out, girlfriend. Come around the counter and sit in my chair. You're not the first one to succumb to the humidity in here. It's beastly."

Gwen jumped over a half swinging door and took H.P.'s arm, guiding her behind the counter and into a surprisingly comfortable padded chair. "Don't move. I'll be right back."

When she returned, she was carrying a paper cup filled with water and a wet washcloth. "Put this one on your neck and the other in your gut. Learned that trick from grad school. Half of our class passed out during the first autopsy."

She felt better almost instantaneously. "I'm not sure what's wrong with me," she whispered.

"I am! You moved to a new place and your grand-mother is haunting you. It's understandable."

"What?" H.P. shot up. "How did you know?"

"That your grandmother's death haunted you? The fact that you weren't able to say goodbye."

"Oh. Right." She eased back down in the chair to allow her body a few more minutes of rest.

"Now, let's get to it. Tell me why you're REALLY here. What is it you want to ask me?"

H.P. studied Gwen's pale, lineless face. There wasn't one ounce of ulterior motive on display. "Just like you, I'm not convinced my grandmother died of natural causes."

Chapter Eight

H.P. slipped on a split pea-colored sweater before entering the walk-in.

One autumn, Gram Gram took a knitting class at Misty Cove Community College. She said it was to relieve her stress, but H.P. knew better. Gram Gram loved to gossip and got little time in-between customers to really dish all the dirt in Misty Cove. Once her book club disbanded, there was no longer a time of day when she could count on seeing friends. She was stuck until closing, when all her friends had settled in at home for the evening.

The sweaters she created, all slightly misshapen, were her pride and joy. H.P. brought the popcorn stitches to her nose and drank in the scent of Gram Gram before donning the sweater and opening the walk-in.

"You might have mentioned your boyfriend was

married, Gram Gram. Now I have to figure out if his wife was the one who... ended your life.

"I'm waiting." H.P. tapped her foot impatiently.

"Let's not bake a fuss-cake, darling. I was lonely. I told you that every time you called."

H.P. resisted the urge to feel hurt that her daily phone calls weren't enough to save her grandmother from falling into the arms of a married man. Many times, she stayed up past her bedtime, listening to Gram Gram's stories of unusual patrons at the diner. "I have to go now, Gram Gram. I've got to be at the restaurant by six a.m.; they've already given me two warnings."

"Just ten more minutes, darling?"

While she understood Edna wasn't much for idle chatter, Gram Gram did spend all day around customers who'd become her friends.

"So, you were lonely. And it didn't occur to you to take up knitting again?" She pulled on the bottom row of the sweater, trying, unsuccessfully, to stretch it into a straight line.

"I tried that. You're wearing the result. Those old hens just cackled on about people I didn't know."

Gram Gram placed her hands on her hips, her earthly signal that she was about to tell a lengthy story.

"Your uncle was what drove me into my lover's arms."

H.P.'s jaw dropped. "You're not saying that you and he—"

"Honeypie Chiffon Sweetwater, I don't know what you're suggesting, but just shove it right out the back door. I meant that when my only remaining son moved out, I started feeling like I was gonna go crazy. After raising my own children and some outstanding grands," she paused to wink at H.P. "it was the first time I'd been alone since your granddaddy ran off. Your Uncle Sebastian kept me company and I thanked him for it."

"Why did he move out, Gram Gram?" H.P.'s heart ached for her grandmother each and every time she heard the story of her grandfather's trip to nearby Piney Falls to purchase a part for the Rise 'n' Shine clock factory, where he was the head of maintenance.

Gramps didn't return for supper, and when the search party didn't find any evidence of him or his car, it was assumed he'd run off.

"You'd have to ask Sebastian. One day, he came home all worked up in a lather. I finally wrestled it out of him; his buddies were coming over the next weekend to move his things."

"And you never asked him why?"

Gram Gram shook her head decisively. "None of my waspwax. He's a grown man, and if he wanted to live somewhere else, he had that right."

Uncle Bash was her champion when there weren't any in the family. Though H.P. remembered them arguing constantly, they must've found common ground. At least for a while.

"Where did you meet your... man?"

"Oh, child." Gram Gram chuckled softly. "You young folks don't understand the art of dating. All of this online whoopsie doodle has taken away your ability to meet new folks."

It was the exact same lecture she'd given Dex. It didn't feel as good when it was directed at her.

"He was hired as a consultant for a local law firm. Lem's retired, but he was bored, so he offered to help others. That's my Lem. Always trying to help others."

"Wait—is this the same lawyer who missed your funeral?"

"One and the same."

"That still doesn't explain how you two hooked up. And it's really not advisable to sleep with the guy who's writing your will."

Gram Gram gasped. "That sounds so tawdry. Jeepers! He came by for lunch every day at two p.m., after the lunch rush and before the kids got off school. We had such good talks about the world."

As unlikely as her romance seemed, H.P. could actually feel the love emanating from her grandmother.

"After months of our chitter-chattering, we both realized we had something special."

"Gram Gram, Gwen told me that your boyfriend was... married."

"He was. That's why I didn't tell any of the family. But you know how small towns are. Word got around quicker than a rat up a drainpipe. Didn't matter that his wife left him decades earlier."

H.P. breathed a sigh of relief.

"It felt good to have someone by my side again. We went to the movies and took long Sunday drives. I missed companionship. He told me numerous times that he wanted to divorce his wife and take things with us more seriously, before..."

"Where can I find this, Lem? I'd like to meet him."

"If he hasn't been in for lunch, I'd guess he left town after my death. Poor man; he must be devastated."

"I wish you'd told me sooner. I wouldn't have judged you, and maybe we could have come up with a way for you to tell the rest of the family together."

"You were in the middle of your own fiasco fiesta and I didn't want to make your life harder. It's time for checkers with Mr. Roosevelt. He's such a cheater. I'll see you again soon, Hun Bun."

H.P. fought back tears as she walked home. Gram Gram kept her heartbreak to herself every night when they spoke. And H.P. droned on and on about her job, or her son, or whatever trivial problem was on her mind.

As a kid, she never gave it a second thought. Grandpa left and Gram Gram carried on as if nothing had happened. She insisted one grandchild spend the night with her every weekend, and from there, kept collecting grandchildren. Her home was always full of laughter, arguments, and energy. It all made sense now.

"Where have you been, Mom?"

Dex banged his palms on the counter, causing Gram Gram's ceramic cookie jar to jiggle.

"I'm here now, bud. Do you want to order a pizza? The place around the corner used to be pretty good."

He sighed with frustration. "You didn't answer your phone. I tried calling four times!"

She pulled her phone out of her purse to find seven unplayed messages.

"I'm so sorry, bud. I've got to do better. The service inside the cooler isn't great."

Dex's eyes showed hurt and betrayal. "You want me to believe you were just hanging out in the cooler? For an hour? Geez, and you lecture me about honesty?"

"I was taking inventory." H.P. turned away from her son to avoid his suspicion, just like he did when he came home late. "What was so important? Is it about that cute girl you brought in the other day? I like her!"

Dex jumped off his stool and spun her around before grasping her face with two long sets of fingers, fingers he'd definitely inherited from Eliot's concert pianist mother. "Mom, this is important. Really important."

"Tell me!" she demanded through squished cheeks. Whoever decided that it was just girls who lived in a world of drama was dead wrong.

"It's Dad. He called today. He's coming here."

"What?" She pulled Dex's hands away from her face and brought them down to his sides. "Maybe he meant someday, but not right now."

"No, Mom," Dex insisted. "He has business in Seattle. He said you never told him we were moving, so he wants to check in with me and make sure I'm all right.

And Mom, Dad says maybe I can go back to Florida with him!"

Chapter Nine

"Tell me more, bud."

She had to handle every bit of information from Eliot with the delicacy of a fluffy meringue. Though he'd run out on them both, paid child support only sporadically, and failed to keep almost every promise he'd ever made to his son, Eliot Jenkins was still Dex's father.

"He said he'd be here the day after tomorrow and he wants to take me out to dinner. He can only stay overnight, because Juliette misses him."

"Yeah, I'll bet."

"Mom!" Dex protested. "I knew you'd act like this. That's why Dad wants to meet me after school, so he doesn't have to come here and see you."

It hit hard. Harder than she thought it might. The man who'd been her first love, a senior at Whitman College when she was a naïve freshman, the man who promised her the first day they met that he'd never leave her side, now found her mere existence so distasteful that he couldn't stand to spend a few moments in the same room.

"I'm sure you'll have a great time. Just the two of you."

She swallowed hard, doing her level best to keep up this charade of cheerfulness. "Make sure you leave time for homework too. You don't want these new teachers to think you're lazy right out of the gate. Though if they saw your bedroom after just three weeks here, they'd have concerns."

"Where can we go to eat, Mom? This stupid town doesn't have anything!"

"There are four restaurants in town that are pretty good, or so I've heard. One is healthy food, so it's probably a no."

"Oh, I heard about that. Bliss, something-or-other? Tildie went there with her dad. She said it was overpriced stuff she eats at home."

H.P. let out a sigh of relief as she faced her son once more. "Well, I'm sure you and your dad will figure it out."

Dex's face displayed a concerned expression, one she knew all-too-well. "Don't worry, bud. I won't show up 'by accident.' I learned my lesson last time."

"Dad said you always pull stunts like that. He can't even come to visit for one day without you begging him to get back together!"

Anger began its short journey to her mouth. "Hey, I was filling in for the sous chef at Baguette that night!"

she snapped. "How was I supposed to know that the two of you would be there? Had your father not insisted upon talking to the chef who made his cream of mushroom soup too salty, we never would have crossed paths."

This conversation was going nowhere fast. "Get your homework done. I'm exhausted. I'll see you in the morning. Love you, baby boy."

She pulled the door shut as softly as she could, what with the strong emotions surging through her entire body. *Stupid Eliot.* How dare he poison their son's mind!

After changing into her softest, most comforting pajamas, she hopped into bed and opened a bodice ripper. She reached Chapter Nine without a clue who the main characters were and realized it was time to get up. Her conversation with Dex was most likely the culprit. "Gram? Are you here? I could use a friend."

Though part of her still questioned her sanity, H.P. resisted the urge to fall asleep for over an hour, just in case Gram Gram stopped by for a chat.

But nothing happened.

The next day, after a strained breakfast conversation with Dex, she made a frothy latte and handed it to Edna.

Edna placed a hand on either full hip and scowled. "What am I supposed to do with that?"

"Drink it. Gram Gram bought this espresso machine and I can't believe you've never tried anything. You've done such a bang-up job keeping this place afloat. You deserve a few minutes to revel in it, don't you think?"

Edna eyed the mug suspiciously, and then H.P. equally so before bringing the mug to her lips. "That'll do, I s'pose."

"Thank you, Edna." It wasn't exactly a ringing endorsement, but H.P. had to take a compliment in whatever form it came. "I was wondering if you knew anything about Gram Gram's boyfriend."

"Lem?" Edna's voice rose dramatically, throwing H.P. for a loop. "What made you think of him?"

"The other day when I was at the dry cleaners, Gwen mentioned him."

You could hear a pin drop, if you didn't count Edna's slurping.

"Yes. Lemon Thornwood is the man's name. Quite a dapper fella." Edna's face softened in a way H.P. wouldn't have thought physically possible if she hadn't seen it for herself.

"From his first day in town, it was chicken noodle with butterballs, if memory serves. Lem oohed and ahhed over Honey. He said they were the best butterballs he'd had since his mother made them. Secret ingredient was nutmeg, he says. Well, that's all it took to have Honey swooning like a school girl. Quickest way to her heart was to compliment the woman."

She pictured Gram Gram with a blush on her yellowed cheeks as she soaked up his praise. Her own children never complimented her cooking, she told H.P. She talked to them about selling the place and moving to Montana one time. That's when they showed up like lions on the hunt. "You can't sell this place! You're the best cook in town!"

"After that," Edna continued, oblivious to the thick foamy mustache on her upper lip, "Lem came in every day. It didn't matter to him whether it was bean with bacon or tomato. The man loves his soup. And your grandmother? Every time, he had a riddle for Honey. She just ate that up."

"What kind of riddle?"

"Oh, this and that." Edna shrugged, picking up a dishcloth and wiping the counter H.P. spent thirty minutes polishing earlier. It wasn't worth the battle to tell her.

"He said he had a book, and his co-workers had their fill. He was glad Honey liked them."

"So, they bonded over riddles and soup. What else?"

Edna dropped the dishcloth and frowned. "You got somewhere else to be? Don't mean to keep you."

"I apologize. Please continue."

"Like I was saying, he came in at two p.m., like clockwork. Until one day, he didn't show. Well, Honey was fit to be tied.

"I finally convinced her to go to the law offices to talk to him. She was getting underfoot here what with her hand-wringing and lack of waitressing."

Edna gave H.P. the side eye. "She'd already been through it with your grandpappy running off, and then your dad..."

"Could we move on, please? That doesn't sound like my grandmother at all. She was a very proud woman, and begging a man for his attention wasn't her style."

"You haven't been 'round for what—ten years? A soul can change a lot in that time. Her kids were gone, her grandkids rarely came to see her..." Edna gave her another sideways glance.

"We talked on the phone every night!" H.P. protested. "She watched Dex grow up on video calls too!"

"Not the same. She needed human touch. Said so more times than I can count."

H.P. remembered that she needed information more than she needed to be right. Again. It was becoming irritating.

"I can't speak for my cousins. They cut me out of their lives too. But I understand what you're saying. Gram Gram needed company. What happened when she confronted Lem?"

"This is her side of things, but I heard another version too. She cut him a piece of her famous honey pie, after he'd finished his soup, cream of broccoli, if memory serves. Lem was too full for pie so she boxed it up while they chatted. When he left, he forgot to take it with him, so off she goes, a-trotting down the street like she's practicing to be a race horse."

Smooth, Gram Gram.

"Lem took her into a private room and explained he couldn't come in anymore because he was starting to have feelings for her and he didn't want her to be the cause of tongues wagging."

"They wagged anyway," H.P. smirked.

"Are you gonna let me finish?"

"Sorry. Go ahead."

"He told her he was sweet on her, and she came back with 'how funny is that; me right here with a piece of my honey pie in my hands!' Lem confessed he and his wife were estranged and hadn't spoken in years. If Honey didn't mind that and wanted to date him, he'd be a happy man."

"I wish I could have seen her so happy in her last few years. If only life had been different. It's strange that we spoke every night, and she never mentioned him. Not once."

"I don't know anything about that. All's I can tell you is they had themselves a grand time. Every Sunday, they drove somewhere new. Either up the Washington Coast or down the Oregon Coast. She'd come back on Monday with all sorts of stories to tell. Really kicked up their heels." Edna chuckled to herself, as though she'd said something funny.

"Why do I feel there's an 'until' in there?"

"Because there is one. They kicked up their heels until your grandmother got a letter in the mail. It was registered mail, so she had to sign for it. Poor woman opened it and burst into tears."

"How do you know it had anything to do with Lem?"

"I tried leaning over her shoulder to read it but she shoved me away. Pretty sure it came from his wife."

"So, Gram Gram knew he was hiding something. Do you—"

"Think he killed her?"

H.P. was shocked. She hadn't mentioned a word to Edna about her ghostly visitor, nor the ghost's assumptions that her death wasn't natural.

"You're not the only one looking under rocks."

Now she understood. Gwen must've gossiped.

"Well, answer my question. Do you think he killed her?"

"Maybe. He was a no-show at the funeral, but folks said he was too shook up. Word 'round town is that he's still working at that law firm. Coming in every day like nothing ever happened. That seems strange, don't it?"

"Very."

Chapter Ten

She heard voices in the driveway, and it took everything in her not to peek through the curtain. Eliot Jenkins had an unmistakable, deep voice that flowed like molten chocolate. It was rich and velvety, filling the room with a warm, soothing baritone that wrapped around you like a cozy blanket on a cold winter's night. If she'd ever thought about it in detail.

As the front door opened, H.P. quickly returned to folding the towels. It was a neat trick she'd learned from other parents at the PTA meetings. "Just make a mess of your laundry. You can refold that stuff a hundred times while you eavesdrop on your kid. Nobody will be the wiser."

"Mom! We know you're watching us! We saw you in the window."

Sheepishly, she appeared in the breezeway, wiping the corners of her mouth to ensure the lipstick she just applied wasn't smeared. Eliot would comment if it was.

Much to her disappointment, the sight of him still made her heart skip a beat. A tall, lithe man with shoulder-length, curly brown hair and deep-set blue eyes, he looked tanned and relaxed.

She paused before reaching father and son. She didn't trust herself.

"H.P., good to see you!"

His false cheeriness only meant one thing: he had bad news. She glanced at her son, who smiled eagerly. All that the kid wanted was two parents who didn't try to tear each other to shreds every time they met. It didn't seem like an impossible ask.

"Yes, good to see you too, El."

Eliot placed a hand on his son's shoulder. "Could you give your mom and me a few minutes alone?"

"Okay." He paused as he brushed by her, uttering, "Be nice, Mom!"

"I'm always nice!" she protested, knowing there were many times she wasn't, but that was only because Eliot knew how to push her buttons.

She took a deep breath, steeling herself before locking eyes with the green-eyed monster she used to refer to as her Adonis. "So, here on business?"

Eliot nodded. "Something like that."

"How are things in Florida?"

He grunted, a sure sign they weren't going to take a delightful trip down memory lane. "Can we cut the small talk, H.P.? I'm only here for the night, and—"

"Yeah, if you think I believe you just happened to

breeze through town to check on your son, well, I've got a pot of gold waiting for you."

She'd already lost control. Her therapist told her years ago that the only way Eliot won was if she gave him the power to control her emotions.

H.P. took a deep breath before starting over. "What's on your mind, El?"

"I've been a jerk."

H.P. blinked rapidly, assuring she wasn't in the middle of a weird, Thai-fusion-induced bad dream. "What did you say?"

"That I've been a jerk." He reached into the pocket of his tan jacket and pulled out a folded check. "My business is going really well. I know I'm a few payments behind in my child support..."

H.P. bit her tongue. If, by "a few," he meant enough to pay cash for the biggest house in Misty Cove, then yes.

"What brought this on? You've never been one to apologize. I believe you told me once that apologies were for weak people."

Eliot rolled his eyes. "I've grown up a lot since college. I would hope you have as well. And thanks to Juliette, I'm a better man. Anyway, Dexter said you ran into some financial difficulties, and I wanted to help you out. No need to pay me back." He took the folded check he pulled out and held it in the air.

If her head had been a teapot, it would have been whistling until it was hoarse as the steam escaped out the top. "Okay, NOW I get it. Dex sent up the smoke signal. You didn't come to see your son at all; you're here to swoop in and play the savior."

She hated the tears forming in her eyes. Both for their effect on her perfectly applied makeup and the gift of emotional control she was giving him.

"Why do you have to be like that? I'm trying to be nice. Go buy the kid some new shoes and put the rest away for his college if it bothers you so much."

The conversation with Dexter regarding his father passed through her mind. "He asked you to come so you would save him. From me." Her tears had now devolved into full-fledged blubbering. *Ack! Not cool, Honeypie, not cool.*

"Geez, H.P.," Eliot's voice softened, making her cry even harder. "This is why I didn't want to come, but the boy begged, so—"

"So, you're going to take him away to Florida? Is that it?" It was now the type of ugly cry that produces an entire river of snot. She refused to leave the room for tissues, as it would signal defeat.

"I'd love to see the kid more often, but... Juliette already has so much on her plate, what with her ceramics business and the twins' activities. She's worried about what it would do to our family dynamic. You get that, right?"

And that was all it took to end the tears. "You... may... think... you've changed, but there's absolutely nothing different about you, Eliot Jenkins. You're the same, insufferable narcissist." She shoved past him and opened the screen door. "I think it's time for you to leave."

The look on his face was a mix of shock, hurt, and, if she were being honest, the sweet cluelessness of the guy she fell in love with. He placed the folded check on Gram Gram's entryway shelf and stood in silence.

"Maybe you didn't hear me. My son and I will continue to function as we always have, taking care of each other. We don't need you. Don't come back again without giving me a week's notice."

Eliot stood firmly in place, a move, or lack thereof, that really burned her biscuit.

"H.P., what are you doing here? Misty Cove is your history, not your future. You've got a culinary degree, for Pete's sake. Dexter told me you ran out of town without giving him time to say goodbye to his friends. Are you running from the law? There's nothing here for you but misery."

"Goodbye, Eliot!"

She refused to look at him again. This familiar dance was done for now. As he moved at a snail's pace toward his rental car, she called out, "Go back to your real family! We're doing just fine!"

Chapter Eleven

"Ma'am?"

"Oh, sorry. I have a million things on my mind."

Since Eliot's departure, Dex had been surly and unwilling to communicate with his mother. If she asked about his homework, he'd grumble something unintelligible before retreating to his bedroom. Additionally irritating was his habit of taking a plate of whatever he confiscated from the diner, (days later to take on the look of a biology experiment) and she wouldn't see him until breakfast.

Despite Dex's treatment of her, H.P. couldn't bring herself to tell him that Eliot "didn't want to ruin the family dynamic."

"He asked me if you could go back to Florida with him, but I told him no, bud. I need you here, supporting me. This move has been tough and your dad understands."

It was much easier to have him angry with her,

even if it meant he skipped showers just to spite her, than to admit his father didn't want him around.

In addition, Honeypie had been avoiding the walk-in for over a week. Any time she needed something, she'd ask Edna to retrieve it for her.

"What's wrong? Your feet don't move forward?"

There was something about Edna's surly demeanor she was starting to appreciate. And Dex really connected with her, too. Mulling all of this over in her brain left her mute when the legal secretary at the law firm, Fulla, Bunce and Vinegar, asked her repeatedly to state her business.

"Sorry. I was hoping to see Lem—Mr. Thornwood?"

The woman eyed Honeypie suspiciously. "What do you need? He's a very busy man."

"It's about my grandmother. Honeypie Sweetwater?"

The woman's expression immediately softened. "Oh! From the diner! I've heard wonderful things about the food! Did the place change hands after... you know?"

H.P. leaned an elbow on her fancy desk. "I'm running it now, after... you know. I'm her grand-daughter and namesake, Honeypie."

"Well, isn't that something?" The woman rolled away from her desk and slapped her hands on her lap. "I never heard a word, and I always have my nose to the ground when it comes to things going on here in Misty Cove. Let me go check on Mr. Thornwood and see if he has time for you."

She got up from her desk and smoothed her tweed skirt and adjusted her nametag, *Brenda, Here to Serve You!* before disappearing through a series of doors. There was a strange hum in Fulla, Bunce, and Vinegar. It wasn't people talking. At least, she didn't think it was.

Glancing around the large, ridiculously fancy lobby, she noticed four women, the only other humans as far as she could tell. The women were dressed in different shades of the same tweed skirt of her first contact. Pale yellow polo shirts, better suited for men than women, finished their uniforms.

Now she realized they were dictating files into the computer.

"He can see you now, Miss Sweetwater."

H.P. jumped when she saw the Head Yellow Polo Shirt again. "You have a real talent for sneaking up on a person!"

"If you'll follow me, please."

Brenda led her to the very last room. Her stomach was in knots, the same way it was every time she was called to the principal's office in high school. "You were counted absent again, Miss Sweetwater. We don't want to embarrass your grandmother now, do we?"

The man behind the desk was not at all how she'd pictured Lem. Gram Gram was beautiful, but she embraced her wrinkles and grey hair and didn't give fashion a second thought.

Lem stood at a height somewhere between professional basketball player and lighting technician with a posture straight and assured. His hair, a beguiling silver, looked like it had been cut by a coiffeur, the name barbers in the city called themselves to charge an extra fifty dollars a cut. Lem's eyes were a vivid blue, bright and observant.

His face was marked with lines that only served to give him more character and he smelled... well, fantastic. Was it wrong she found Gram Gram's boyfriend a bit—hot?

Not cool, H.P. Not cool.

"Miss Sweetwater? Please, have a seat." He motioned toward a plush leather chair across from his desk. Though it was a small office, every piece of furniture looked like it came from a European furniture store that served coffee, just daring you to spill.

Holding his tie, he sat down and motioned to her to do the same. He was studying her face, too. Probably looking for similarities to Gram Gram. Unfortunately, there were very few. "You look like your mother's side, Hun Bun. Don't worry, there are all sorts of creams and such to help when you get older."

"What can I do for you today?"

She raised one brow, unsure why he didn't already know. "I... heard about you and my grandmother. I needed to..."

"To see what we had in common?" He chuckled and leaned back in his chair, swiveling toward the window and then back again. "She was an amazing woman. Just amazing. I was lucky to spend this last year with her."

Honeypie wanted to ask a hundred questions, but she had to play this carefully. "What was she like when you were together? I only know her as my caretaker and the owner of a successful business."

"She was the best." He leaned his head against his headrest and fingered his tie. "When her husband left to buy parts for the factory and never returned, it nearly broke her. She and her three daughters—"

"And my Uncle Bash!" H.P. didn't bother naming her own father, since that was a sore subject around town. People who weren't old enough to know about her grandfather knew about her father running off and didn't take kindly to it.

"Apologies. Your uncle urged Honeypie to start the diner with old family recipes. He'd watched his father bury money in the backyard because he didn't believe in banks. Sebastian dug up the money and told his mother to start a diner. It was all his doing, well, and your grandmother's. Did you know that?"

"Of course, I did. Everyone in the family knows that story!"

She'd heard the story in many forms: her own father buried money he procured during a bank robbery, Uncle Bash buried money to keep it away from his second wife; there were many. The remaining family members came out the nicest in this version.

"Even with the money to start her business, folks in town thought she'd fail. Well, she proved them wrong, didn't she? I told her I'd love to write her life story and incorporate our love story. What a book, right?"

This small talk wasn't getting them anywhere. "Mr. Thornwood, I didn't come to discuss our family history. I'm here to find out if my grandmother had any enemies that you know of? Anyone who might want to cause her harm?"

In one motion, he leaned forward and clasped his hands together and cocked his head to the side. "Why would you ask? She was beloved by every single person she met. She gave to the food drive every year and never turned a hungry traveler away when they showed up on her doorstep."

"I... I just didn't want any surprises. You know how small towns are. Someone might come into the diner and expect I know about their feud with Gram Gram."

"Oh. Right."

Lem resumed his relaxed position, leaning back in his fancy chair. "No, she was a lovely woman in every way and her standing in the community reflected that. She bragged about her grandchildren and great grandchildren to anyone who listened. We were planning a trip to San Francisco to visit you and your son."

Not once during their phone calls had Gram Gram mentioned this. When she'd encourage a visit to San Francisco, she always refused.

"Please, Gram Gram? Dex only knows you from photos and video calls. He needs to meet the woman who raised me."

"Hun Bun, I need to get out of Misty Cove, but I just

can't leave the diner. And to be honest, I'm content right here."

"Did she mention anything more current? Anything that seemed odd?"

"She didn't tell me your deepest, darkest secrets, if that's what's worrying you."

Lem winked at H.P. as though he were speaking to a child.

"But she did tell you about my father?"

"Because it hurt her so deeply. Your coming to live with her helped heal that wound. Did she ever tell you that?"

"Uh-huh."

Clearly, Lem had ALL of Gram Gram's life stories and he wasn't going to stop until she was begging for mercy.

"I should have framed that differently. She always spoke very highly of you and your son. The fact that you called her every night meant everything. She'd brag about the fancy restaurants you were working in. The last time I was in San Francisco on business, I made reservations at Gleu, hoping to see you."

Her cheeks must've turned the color of her home-made ketchup. "I was only there for three months. The head chef and I had a difference of opinion."

He wanted their working relationship to include after-hours benefits, and she did not. Now that the focus was on her, H.P. felt distinctly uncomfortable. "Gwen, over at the dry cleaners said you... um... found her."

Lem's bright smile faded. "I did indeed. We were going to plan out a Sunday drive for the next day, so I brought croissants and coffee."

His eyes darted back and forth quickly and, if she weren't mistaken, became a little teary.

"When I knocked and rang the bell with no response, I walked around to the side of the house, where I found an open window. Now, that wasn't out of the ordinary for your grandmother. She liked her bedroom to resemble an ice block when she slept."

H.P. shivered, both at the thought of Gram Gram in a cold room, foreshadowing her end, and the fact that Lem knew this intimate detail.

"I heard about the open window. I understand that Gram liked to keep things cool, but might there have been any signs of a forced entry? Signs of a struggle?"

Lem's professional demeanor was starting to melt away as he shook his head, fighting back tears. "The woman I loved was lying on the floor, dead. That's what I saw. The rest is a matter for the police."

"You found her... you found her..." H.P.'s own voice wavered with emotion. "Beside her bed? With the scissors, and, you know."

She couldn't bear to picture what had happened. The thought of her grandmother suffering in any way was too much.

Lem nodded, struggling to fight to keep his own emotions in check. "A basket of yarn sat on the bed, along with a half-done potholder. She did love her crafts. But for them to be her undoing? Never in a million years would I have guessed."

She stared hard at this man who seemed like a very convenient enemy. "I was also told that you're married."

Without missing a beat, he replied, "Yes, I made no secret of the fact that Agnes and I hadn't finalized our divorce." He leaned forward and clasped his hands in front of him on his desk, back in professional mode. "You know the saying, 'Physician, heal thyself?' It's meant to infer that doctors are their own worst patients. I believe the same can be said of attorneys. We don't do a good job of regulating our legal obligations."

She wasn't going to let this one pass. "How long were you estranged from your wife?"

"Fifteen years. Agnes lives in Maryland now. The last time I saw her, we crossed paths in the Denver airport. We had coffee, quite congenial. It became apparent we'd both made the right decision."

"But you didn't discuss divorce? So, you could be with the love of your life?"

"Miss Sweetwater, your grandmother and I didn't have a conventional relationship. We enjoyed each other's company, but there were no expectations. That's what made it work for us both."

Here, too, was another discrepancy in the information she'd gathered. "Let me get this straight. My grandmother was the love of your life, but you weren't in a serious relationship." The volume of her voice grew louder and more accusatory with each phrase. "You didn't bother to look around the crime scene for anything suspicious, and you STILL hung out with dear, old Agnes? Did I get that right? All of this and you were the guy who wrote out her will. Sounds a little fishy, doesn't it?"

"You're twisting my words, Miss—"

"Unfortunately, Mr. Thornwood, I've met a number of men like you. Have your cake and eat it too, right? My poor Gram Gram, she was lonely, and you took advantage of that, didn't you? Is that why you weren't at her funeral?"

H.P. knew she should stop, but the hate just kept pouring out of her mouth. She needed someone to blame for Gram Gram's death, and today, that was Lem Thornwood.

"No, I was looking after a neighbor. I can assure you; I planned every detail with several of your cousins. You might ask them if you want to know about the service. I hear it was so full, they had to open up the Bison Club meeting room to accommodate everyone."

He was doing his best to calm her down, but it was having the opposite effect. "And her will? Why is it sealed? Because of your underhanded games? What ACTUALLY happened, Mr. Thornwood? You found a lonely lady who had a nice nest egg that you could use to woo your wife back?"

"I didn't write her will, Miss Sweetwater."

There was an unwanted knock on the door. "Excuse me, I just wanted to make sure things were going okay. Can I get you something to drink, Miss Sweetwater?"

"I don't need anything to drink," H.P. snapped, irritated at this feeble attempt to calm her. "What I do need is for this guy to be honest and admit he took advantage of my grandmother! Maybe he even KILLED HER!!!"

A tweed-skirted woman paused as she was walking by Lem's office, leaning in to listen.

H.P. turned in her chair, shocked to find a gorgeous man in an expensive suit standing behind her. Petite with dark curly hair, he smiled with genuine kindness. His skin was a smooth, light caramel tone, complimenting his striking features. His face was sculpted with high cheekbones and a strong jawline covered by a hint of a beard. His eyes, a deep, warm brown, were expressive and conveyed more than his soft-spoken words did.

She'd dated another sous chef from Study, a trendy restaurant in the alley adjacent to her condo, for three years before realizing he was also dating the sous chef from Nothin But Ribz.

"I'm, um..."

"Mr. Thornwood is just visiting, so he doesn't know as much about the locals as I do. I don't have another client until three. Would you like to go for coffee? There's a great place right across the street."

Almost every ounce of her wanted to stand her ground, but it was that quarter cup of butter that did all the talking. "Okay." She rose and glared at Lem

Thornwood. "But I'm not done with you yet, Mr. Thornwood."

"My door is always open, Miss Sweetwater. As long as we can speak civilly to one another." He nodded before giving the handsome stranger a look that said, "I'll owe you a beer after work."

As they stepped outside, H.P. looked up to see if it was raining. Instead, she saw Lem Thornwood staring out of a window with a phone pressed firmly to his head. When he realized she was watching him, he turned abruptly.

They walked in silence. Of course, this Adonis didn't want to say anything, she reasoned. This gorgeous creature was afraid she'd verbally batter him, too.

"My treat today," he said as they stood in a long line. "They make a mean Foggy Frap. It's their version of a frozen mocha. Not exactly on my diet, so I only allow myself one per week."

She glanced around, searching for an open table. "Get me one too. I see a table in the corner."

While she waited, admiring him from afar, her phone buzzed. "Tildie asked me over. It's no big deal, so don't make it one."

"Aww. Okay, bud. Don't be late for dinner. Mac and cheese with smoked salmon, your favorite."

As she hung up, the handsome lawyer returned to the table.

"You must've received good news?" His soft-spoken voice caught her off guard. In the world of professional chefs, everyone had a harsh urgency to everything they spoke.

"It's my son. We've only been here a month, and he's already found himself a little girlfriend. His first."

"It's so hard not to live vicariously through them, isn't it? My kids are always trying to make me work for it when it comes to their happiness. I'm just assuming—"

"You assumed right. Teen boys are not for the faint of heart. And I don't believe we've been formally introduced. I'm Honeypie Sweetwater. My friends call me H.P."

She offered her hand across their drinks. When it touched his, she felt two things: his buttery-soft skin, and then an unwanted electricity that ran from the top of her head to her toes.

No. Nope. We're not getting involved. Once this whole murder situation is resolved, we're moving on.

"I'm Abraham. My friends call me Abe, my parents call me 'a waste of a presidential name,' and my kids are another matter."

They both chuckled before taking drinks of the frothy, chocolaty concoction.

"Honeypie Sweetwater, after my Gram. But everyone calls me H.P. How many kids do you have, Abe?"

"Two—a son and a daughter. My son decided to live with my wife after the divorce, so it's just me and my daughter right now."

"I'm sorry. That's gotta bite. I had the opposite

problem. My ex ran off and barely remembers he HAS a son. Do you know how many birthday and Christmas presents I bought and put his name on them? It's a delicate balancing act. I vacillate between trying to let him figure out his father is a slug and trying to make sure he doesn't fall victim to said slug."

Abe grinned, showcasing the most amazing mouth of straight white teeth she'd ever seen. H.P. didn't try hiding her admiration. Something about the way he looked at her made her want to tell him every last detail of her life.

She almost did.

When she realized she had to use the restroom, she glanced first at her empty cup and then at the clock. "Four-thirty? How is it so late? I'm sorry, Abe. I doubt I could afford whatever you'd charge your clients for a conversation of this length!"

He laughed like a gentle breeze. It made her wish she had something actually funny to say.

"I get it now. You're trying to distract me with your boyish charm so that I don't remember I wanted to skewer Mr. Thornwood."

"What's got you so upset with him? If you don't mind my asking?"

He rested his chin on his palm and stared soulfully into her eyes.

"Um... he..." It was hard to stay focused. "My grandmother was in a relationship with him. He didn't even bother to come to her funeral."

"Oh, I see. Well, I can put your mind at ease. Lem

is a good guy. He came out of retirement to help our firm with a tough case, and we convinced him to stay on. He never says no when he's asked to help. If I'm not mistaken, Lem made all the arrangements for your grandmother's service. He'd planned to arrive early for the service, but his neighbor's car was stolen. Poor, little, old lady who didn't know what to do, and she begged Mr. Thornwood to stay with her."

"Oh." How had she been so wrong about this guy? Or maybe Mr. Good Teeth was making it up as he went?

"If you'll excuse me, I've got to take this." Abe stood and brought his phone to his ear without any indication that it rang.

She sat in her thoughts, feeling ugly as he walked away. What Abe must think of me? Why do I care? He's nobody to me.

Abe returned to the table with a sober expression on his face. "I'm sorry, I have to return to the office. A rather needy client is having an emergency." He nodded as though Honeypie understood. She nodded back, even though she didn't.

"I hate to leave you here alone."

"Go!" she made a pushing motion with her hand and felt relieved she wouldn't have to sit with him and wonder what he was thinking of this self-centered woman.

Chapter Twelve

"Edna, what do you know about Lem Thornwood?"

Edna didn't bother looking up as she swept the pie crumbs an unruly toddler left behind. "Why?"

She was becoming the most irritating woman H.P.'d ever met. And that included the owner of Fists Bistro, who took steroids and periodically paid her staff to sit and listen to her scream for an hour.

H.P. had only known Edna as a child, and as such, she stayed out of Edna's way. Now that they were both older and set in their ways, Edna's attitude became insufferable.

"Because he was the last person to see my grandmother!" She let her temper get the better of her. "And if you really want to know, I'm the only one who seems to care that my grandmother was murdered!"

Edna leaned the broom against a table and stared at Honeypie with her dull, brown eyes. "First I've heard of it. She fell on her scissors and bled out peacefully. We should all be so lucky."

H.P. gave her co-worker a look of exasperation. "You said the other day that you thought she was murdered too! What is it with everyone in this town? Can't a single one of you tell the truth?"

Basil popped his head out of the kitchen door. "Everything all right?"

"Nothing to worry about, Basil. Edna and I are having a little difference of opinion, is all."

He didn't move until Edna nodded in agreement, which made H.P. even more upset. "We're FINE, Basil!"

Edna moved to another corner of the diner, with Honeypie following close behind. "Gram Gram was murdered. I'm sure of it. And Lem's the number two suspect, that is, after you, Edna."

Edna sighed with irritation as she dropped the broom and placed a fist on either hip. "Don't keep me in suspense. What's got you thinkin' I'm a murderer?" She shook her head slowly back and forth without moving her neck. "Honestly, if I didn't know any better, I'd think your grandmother was speaking through you. Once that woman got an idea into her head, it stuck harder than bubblegum on a hot side-walk in July."

"You had a motive to kill her. You've worked here for as long as she did. Maybe she told you she was leaving the diner to me, so you got your revenge."

The next sound she heard was so unexpected, so

abrupt, and so bizarre that she thought about it for a week solid.

It was a cackle that was both high-pitched and raspy, punctuated by unexpected snorts. Its irregular, varying tempo, sometimes fast and giddy, other times slow and wheezy had no logical rhythm.

Edna was laughing.

The more she heard it, the more she thought it sounded like an injured animal. In fact, if Honeypie hadn't been staring directly into the face of the surly woman who called comedy, "the surest way to scoop out your soul," she wouldn't have believed that sound and laughter were related.

"Honeypie Chiffon, you've got a good imagination on you. Sit." Edna motioned to a booth that hadn't been cleaned yet.

"Why don't we sit over here?" Honeypie gestured the other direction, to a sanitized booth.

"Because I already cleaned there, that's why. Don't want customers to sit down and think they're in a clean space when it isn't. Your sass level hasn't changed, I'm sorry to say."

Reluctantly, Honeypie plopped down in the dirty booth across from Edna. Edna brought a clean cloth with her and wiped away tiny fingerprints and dried ketchup.

"I'm listening, Edna. Explain why I shouldn't suspect you of my grandmother's murder."

"You know that the two of us worked side-by-side for nigh thirty years. What you don't know is that we helped each other through ugliness. Your dad's disappearance, for one."

"I would imagine you were a great comfort to her."

"It wasn't comfort, it was tit for tat. When my husband and son died in a car accident, she came over every day with food, or whatever I needed. Didn't want me to come back to work until I was ready, so she paid all my bills for six months. I barely got out of my negligee, but I did recover."

While it sounded exactly like something Gram Gram would do, it was still shocking to hear, because Gram Gram never made any mention of Edna's tragedy, or what she'd done to help her, or the cringe-worthy idea of Edna wearing a negligee.

"I'm so sorry, Edna. That must've been very hard for you."

Edna nodded and wrapped her knuckles on the table. "It was. I don't like thinking about it anymore. The only reason I brought it up was to give you an example of what we did for each other. Which brings me to my point."

Edna brought her elbows to the table and leaned forward; the pot of coffee she'd drunk during the course of the day was evident by the strong scent on her breath. "Don't you think your grandmother would have offered the place to me first?"

Honeypie sat back, contemplating those words. "I didn't... of course she did. She asked if you wanted the business, and you said no."

Edna smiled, thumping her own head. "Now

you're using your noggin. One of these days, I'm gonna retire and take Mother to Canada. She's always wanted to see the Mounties."

It was hard to know what to process first: the fact that Edna was interested in travel, or that her mother was still alive. Edna seemed ancient, for as long as Honeypie knew her.

"Right. That certainly makes sense." There was no way to exit this conversation without an awkwardness between them. "Let's finish cleaning and get out of here. Dex is home alone, and—"

"Who else are you harassing? You said you're taking me off the list. Who else is on this so-called list? Is it a popularity thing? Or is it more of a first-come-first-serve type of thing?"

H.P. shook her head. "I've got some ideas about what really happened to Gram Gram. I would hate to implicate someone who turned out to be just as innocent as you are, Edna. We wouldn't want to alienate anyone, would we?"

She hoped that would be the end of it. After all, even though Edna was off the list, it didn't mean she wasn't involved in some convoluted plot to take over the diner.

"Don't drive yourself off a bridge, trying to prove something that isn't there."

"I understand why you didn't want the diner, but why did she leave it to me? I hadn't seen her in years, and I wasn't even able to attend the funeral. I've got scads of cousins who would have jumped at the chance to put their spin on this place."

She remembered how her cousin, Paisley always bragged that she would run the diner when she was older and how she would develop her own line of pies, based on her own recipes, not Gram Gram's.

"Can't tell you."

Edna got up and turned her body away from Honeypie.

"Why not?"

"Strict instructions from your grandmother. Not until the time is right."

H.P.'s phone rang at the worst possible moment. Looking down, she realized she had to take it. "Hey, bud! Edna and I are just finishing up. Do you want me to pick up a pizza on the way home?"

"Mom, you've got to come home." His still-babyish voice wavered. "Dad's in trouble!"

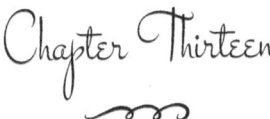

Chapter Thirteen

"Juliette hasn't heard from him since he left last weekend."

Honeypie suppressed a grin. Yes, she was that petty person who took joy in the misery of another. Well, mostly just the misery of Juliette, but still... "Maybe he needed a little time to himself. You know your father; he doesn't feel the need to announce it when he takes a little break from life."

"Mom! This isn't about you! Geesh!"

Dex turned his head away from her, a new behavior he used to keep her from observing the flow of emotion running down his cheeks.

"Hey!" She took his chin gently in her fingers and turned it to face her. With her other sleeve, she wiped his tears away. "It's okay to cry. You're a human and we all feel pain."

"Well, you don't."

Her heart hurt hearing those words. "Why do you say that, son? Of course I feel pain!"

"You moved us away from home without saying goodbye to any of your friends. You didn't even come to Gram Gram's funeral or feel sad about it. You hate Dad. If you feel pain, I've never seen it."

The irony of fighting back her tears as she tried convincing her son she had feelings was not lost on Honeypie Chiffon Sweetwater. She swallowed hard before she spoke. "When I was a kid, I was a loner, an outsider."

"And everyone picked on you. I know this story!"

"Just let me finish, please." She took a moment to compose herself, in order to tell this story in just the manner it deserved. "You know my mom ran off with the pizza delivery guy. And then—"

"Your dad disappeared when you were ten and you went to live with Gram Gram. You've told me all of this, Mom!"

Dex took the opportunity to wipe his nose on his shirt, a move that was sure to evoke anger from her.

H.P. didn't take the bait. Her eyes grew distant as she delved deeper into her memories, her voice taking on the cadence of a story told many times over in the quiet of her own mind. "I was nine, actually. My father wasn't a great guy, but he read fairy tales to me before bed. When he left me, I fantasized that life with Gram Gram would be exactly like those stories. As much as I loved her... well, she was more like hard candy—sweet, but tough to crack."

She paused, a shadow crossing her face. "One day, she took me to the park, the one by the old mill where the other kids played. She told me to go make friends while she read her newspaper on the bench. I tried; I really did. But I was the new girl, the odd one out, and the other kids, they just... they wouldn't let me in. I remember the laughter, not the warm kind, but the kind that slices through you like a cold wind."

Dex remained blessedly silent, allowing her the space to continue.

"I spent that whole afternoon sitting by the pond, feeding the ducks and pretending I didn't care. But I did. And every once in a while, I glanced back at Gram Gram, hoping she might come over and take me into her arms and give me a big hug. Instead, she just nodded and smiled, like it was all just part of growing up in her eyes. Losing both my parents didn't compare to how alone I felt that day."

H.P.'s voice cracked slightly. "She never knew how much that hurt, how much I needed her to... just be there, to tell me it was going to be okay. And when she passed, all the unspoken words between us, all the hugs we never shared, they just stayed inside me, like a lump of coal I couldn't swallow."

"That's why you didn't go to her funeral?" Dex's voice rose an octave.

Honeypie nodded, a tear finally escaping. "Because if I had gone, all that pain, and all the loneliness, would've come out. And I wasn't ready to let it go, not yet. I thought I could carry it, that it would get lighter with time."

She looked at her son with glistening eyes. "But some things, they don't get lighter, they just... stay heavy. And you have to find a way to carry them."

Dex reached out, taking her hand. "Maybe we can carry it together."

And in that simple gesture, Honeypie felt the weight she had borne for so long shift, becoming just a little more bearable.

The room fell quiet, except for the occasional sniffle from Dex and the distant chirping of crickets outside the window. Honeypie continued, her voice a soft murmur. "When I went to live with Gram Gram, she told me she knew I was hurting, and I acted tough, like nothing could touch me. But inside, I was like one of those chocolate Easter bunnies—all hollowed out. I thought your dad was the answer to my hurt. I tried molding him into the person I needed, but it was like trying to reset an old watch."

Dex looked up, his eyes wide with a mixture of sadness and understanding. "I wish you would have told me this when Dad first left."

"You were still a baby of six! There was no way I would lay all of this on your shoulders. I feel guilty even telling you today!"

Her son, her world, started at the floor. "I may not show it, but I've mastered the art of crying on the inside—like a champ."

A giggle erupted from the mass of curls hiding her

son's face. "That's the saddest attempt at humor I've ever heard."

Honeypie ruffled his hair. "Well, I did win third place in the 'Miss Sad Humor Pageant' of '89."

"And what happened to first and second place?" Dex asked, already knowing the answer to their often-repeated joke.

"Disqualified for smiling during the 'Cry Me a River' talent portion of the pageant."

Dex's laughter blossomed into a full-blown, deep-throated laugh. The sound mingled with the softness of the night, as Honeypie joined in, their shared amusement a balm on the open wounds of their hearts. And for a moment, just a fleeting moment, the hollow chocolate bunnies inside them felt a little less empty.

Chapter Fourteen

"Gram Gram?

"It took a major effort to get here before seven. I had to promise Dex a pie of his choosing, most likely marionberry, that he could eat in his room."

She shuddered as she pictured the mess of crumbs, purple berries, and possibly ants that she'd find next week when she gave up on him changing his own bed sheets.

As H.P. paced back and forth, back and forth in the walk-in, she glanced at her watch. 6:35 a.m. Edna would be here in another ten minutes, and then she'd be forced to explain her presence in the cooler after avoiding it for so many days. It was a wonder that the perennial sharp-as-a-tack Edna Snarlwood hadn't caught on to the fact that something wasn't right yet. Nobody spent that much time in a walk-in cooler for no reason.

"Land sakes, child. What's got your whoopsie in a doodle?"

The sweet scent of her grandmother's ghost did nothing to calm H.P.'s irritation today.

"You have all of eternity to play chess with the pope, or teach Marilyn Monroe how to knit. I'm still on the living side of the universe and I need you!"

"All right, all right. I'm listening." Gram Gram's ethereal image floated closer to her granddaughter.

"I went to see your boyfriend. Lem Thornwood is an irritating man, Gram Gram. I'm sorry, but he's a smooth talker and I have no doubt that he swindled you in some way. You deserved better."

Gram Gram smacked her lips repeatedly. "What I'm hearing is that you found him bothersome, but you don't suspect him of murder?"

H.P. rolled her eyes. "I don't know WHAT to think. Why didn't he come to your funeral? I don't buy the 'doing a good deed' angle."

"If I knew that, I wouldn't be asking you to investigate, child."

"In any case, he's on the back burner for now. This whole town is full of people hiding something, if memory serves. I hate to change my plans, though."

The truth was, she didn't have a timeline for moving on. The bank should have utilized the full resources of the governor (wasn't that how it worked?) to find her by now.

"Have you been to visit Maddysin yet?"

She'd detoured to Lem's office instead of visiting Maddysin. "Today, on my break. I promise."

"Gram Gram, Lem mentioned a window that was open when he found you. Do you remember if you opened it?"

Gram touched her chin repeatedly as she thought. "I loved the fresh air, Hun Bun. Spending so much of my life inside the diner, I always kept a window cracked when I was home, just to smell that lovely ocean breeze."

"Was there anyone besides Lem who knew your window was always open?"

Gram Gram giggled. "Are you asking me if it was a topic of conversation? 'Mrs. Sweetwater, I love your cooking, and oh, by the way, do you leave your windows open?' Do you mean like that?"

"I guess that didn't make sense, did it?" H.P. realized this was getting her nowhere, so she decided to change course.

"If I'm going to see Maddysin, I need to make sure there are no surprises. Did you have any other interactions with Maddysin? Something that might make her uncomfortable?"

Okay, girlfriend, that's totally for your entertainment, not for finding Gram Gram's killer.

"None that I can think of... other than the time she broke in."

"What? How did she get in?"

"The girl has connections, you know. Her uncle, Max Gridley, owns the power company. They have master keys to every residence in town. When you go over to her fancy spa, ask her about it. Oh, dear. You've got company."

H.P. opened the door so fast, she almost slipped on the cement floor getting out of the cooler.

"Edna, I came in early to—"

"I'm the anti-Edna."

Looking up, H.P. was relieved to see her friend. "Gwen! How did you know I'd be here so early?"

"Your grandmother was always here before six, making pies or cinnamon rolls or something. I thought you probably continued that tradition."

"Yes! I sure did!"

The blush on her cheeks was nothing compared to the inner blush she felt for not actually coming in early to bake. "What brings you to the diner?"

"When you were at the cleaners the other day, you mentioned that you thought your grandmother was murdered."

H.P. stared into Gwen's earnest face. If she were going to find the killer, she'd need to do a better job of keeping things to herself. "Right. I'm sure that isn't true. You know how we get emotional after a loved one passes, and our minds play tricks on us? I'm sure that's what happened to me."

"Oh."

"But if you have some new information, I'd be willing to listen."

Gwen pulled an envelope out of her navy jacket pocket. "I didn't want to tell you the other day because

I was slightly ashamed. But I've asked around, and you're a good egg, it seems."

"Okay..." H.P. replied cautiously, still uncertain of the direction this was taking.

"I performed an autopsy on your grandmother. I was suspicious that her death wasn't natural. I can't tell you why. I know Lem and he's a decent guy, and if he says she tripped and fell on the scissors, I should believe him."

"But..."

"But, I guess it was more of my coroner's intuition."

"What happened to make you think he wasn't telling the truth?"

"It wasn't about Lem, so much. He was sincerely upset when he found her. I guess I wondered if someone else had been in the house that they didn't find?" Gwen turned away from H.P. before uttering, "Bad Gwen! Bad Gwen!"

H.P. waited quietly. She'd discovered with every human over twenty, it worked like magic to obtain information, but as Gwen continued berating herself, it was time to step in. "Okay, Gwen. You've gotten up early and brought me an important-looking document. Time to lay all of your cards on the table."

H.P. reached across the counter for the folder, but Gwen jerked it back at the last minute.

"Wait. Before you see it, I need to tell you something else."

H.P. glanced up at the clock. Edna would arrive at

any moment, and she had a knack for finding H.P. at the most inopportune times. "We're about to open, so..."

"Right. Your grandmother had a mix of formaldehyde, petroleum distillates, and p-dichlorobenzene in her system."

Edna came through the front door and stopped in her tracks. "Was there a store meeting? Or is this some kind of millennial drug party? You kids and your weird habits."

"None of the above. And I'll choose to feel flattered that you think of me as a millennial. Gwen was just here ordering a pie."

Gwen's face twisted into a mixture of shock and panic.

"Your mother wants another Choconut Cream? That woman can put away the meringue like no one I've ever seen."

Edna set her lunch bag on the counter while she took off her coat. "I'll put that on the schedule. What day did you want to pick it up?"

"I..."

"Gwen and I are meeting for drinks on Thursday. I told her I'd bring it then."

Edna eyed them both suspiciously. "I don't trust this little gathering. Remember that when you think I'm not listening."

She picked up her lunch and marched through the swinging doors.

"My mother is on a diet. She told me she'd throw

away my favorite summer suit if I brought home another pie," Gwen hissed, in a voice barely above a whisper. "I'll have to give it to my dad at his office. Geesh, you lie like you've done it before!"

Seizing the opportunity, H.P. grabbed the file away from Gwen and began reading. "What did all of those words mean?" H.P. whispered, ignoring Gwen's concerns. "In English?"

"Air freshener, injected between her toes. It was enough to effectively paralyze her. Your grandmother most likely tried to get out of bed and rolled onto the floor."

"And on top of the scissors? How convenient for the killer. We're looking for a crafter with knowledge of solutions that produces paralysis. Sounds like a breeze."

Chapter Fifteen

Cinnamon Biscuit Maker stretched a paw forward and rested her head on H.P.'s lap. "Cinnie, you're a hard girl to refuse." H.P. stroked her soft white-and-black fur, feeling comforted by the strong vibration of the sweet kitty's purr.

Her assumption that the cat camped out in front of the diner was male turned out to be wrong. "Ms. Sweetwater, my apologies for being so forward," Tildie began, "but I checked, and the little cat you adopted is actually a girl."

Dex insisted on naming her, even as H.P. protested that she might already have a family. "We've never had a pet, Mom, even though you promised! Please let me name her?"

Buying gourmet cat food (Dex and Tildie researched and found the healthiest—translation—most expensive cat food at the store) was the second thing on her "that will never happen" life list. The first was talking to a ghost in the walk-in cooler. Or anywhere, for that matter.

As if on cue, Cinnie's motor revved up as she thwapped the kitchen table with her tail. "You're giving this all you've got, little girl, aren't you?"

With Eliot's newfound influx of cash, maybe he would agree to transport the cat across the country, so that Dex could at least see her on summer breaks.

Petting her temporary cat in her temporary lodging as she paid the bills made for a nice diversion, but the truth was, the money in Gram Gram's business account was dwindling. Though the diner was making money, it wasn't enough to get ahead. It didn't make any sense. When she went over the books, it appeared they should be rolling in cash.

"Edna, can you take a look at these figures and make sure I didn't do something wrong?"

The handwritten ledger book had multiple coffee stains on the cover and smiley face stickers on almost every page.

"Do I look like an accountant to you?" Edna leaned against the door frame, folding her arms over her chest.

"You've been doing these books ever since Gram died, right? I see profits every month. But when I look at what's left in the bank account—"

"You'll figure things out." Edna turned to leave and continued the conversation as she shuffled down the short hall to the kitchen. "Otherwise, your grand-mother never would have left this place to you."

Great. Before long, she'd be a failure in two states.

Her misery was interrupted by Dex, who looked—and smelled— surprisingly clean.

"Mom, Tildie and me are going to her place to work on our team speech after school."

"What kind of speech?"

"Mom—"

"You know, I was in the drama club in high school. I could give you some pointers."

"NO! Stop, Mom! You never listen!" he huffed. "We're not actors, it's a contest to see who can write and perform the best speech to represent our school in a district-wide contest. We're doing this for a grade. And it's a made-up commercial for a made-up product. No big deal."

"What product?"

Dex walked to the front door, ignoring his mother. "See you for dinner!"

At least he was feeling more comfortable. He hadn't complained about being the new kid in over a week. Tildie seemed like a sweet girl. She certainly had a positive influence on Dex.

"Okay, Gram Gram, I'm heading over to the spa this morning. I wouldn't do this for anyone else."

Though Gram Gram was attached to the diner, H.P. had taken to talking to her grandmother every time she was alone. It made H.P. feel safe knowing, or at least thinking, that her beloved grandmother was there, watching over things.

H.P. took advantage of the time it took to drive to the spa and opened all the windows in her car. The ocean air was what she'd missed most about Misty Cove. Though she lived beside the ocean in San Francisco, the only sound she ever heard was the clanging of pans and the bark of impatient chefs.

Tonight, she was meeting Gwen for drinks. Maybe if she got Gwen drunk enough, she could ask her what she knew about otherworldly members of the community?

Maddysin's spa on the outskirts of town was impressive. There were actual palm trees lining the long, curvy driveway up to the three-story, yellow-stuccoed, Spanish-style building. H.P. pulled the visor down to do a quick check in the mirror, just to ensure there were no surprises.

The first unwelcome sight was her unbrushed teeth with bits of a delicious spinach and feta cheese omelet stuck in between. At least she'd remembered to comb her hair. Digging through the glove box, she found a half-eaten candy bar, two left-hand gloves, and finally, a tube of Madly Marionberry lipstick.

A light tap on the window alerted her to the fact that the valet was ready to park her car. She glanced up at the elderly man, dressed in a tan-and-crimson bell hop uniform. "Give me a second!" she shouted through her closed window. H.P. slammed her glove box shut, catching crumpled receipts from The Burger Hatch in the process.

She got out and smoothed her rumpled, black dress before handing the keys over.

The spa had a large sign in front, informing guests they were entering Blissful Bloom Spa and Resort.

"Oh, I get it. You changed your name as a marketing ploy. Good one, Maddysin."

The lobby of the spa was just as opulent as she thought it would be. Enormous crystal chandeliers, six in total, hung throughout the lobby. The music playing was the same kind of new-agey stuff her last boss blasted during employee retreats. It made no sense to her that they stuffed their faces with junk food while they "retreated," but it wasn't her call. Some unusual smell— *was that patchouli and lavender?* Permeated the air.

She walked up to a very long white desk, where three women, all dressed identically in beige suits with tan shirts underneath, said hello simultaneously. As she moved in closer, she observed that each woman sported a mid-back-length ponytail and beige nail polish. In front of them were name plates that read, alternately, "Brandi," "Tandi" and "Randi."

"Pick your check-in, beautiful lady. Let's begin the rest of your life." She eyed them all suspiciously. There were cult movies that began like this.

"I'm just here to see Maddysin."

The women exchanged worried glances.

"If you've got a complaint, we're happy to help you, beautiful—"

"Lady, I know. Just ring her up for me, please. I've got to be at work in a few minutes."

The woman nearest to her gestured for H.P. to

come closer. When she'd reached her space, the woman whispered. "We get docked a day's pay when people register complaints with Bliss. She doesn't like to be disturbed, and she REALLY hates it when she has to deal with customers."

H.P. stuck her tongue in her cheek, forcing her mouth into a neutral position. It gave her way too much happiness; the thought of giving Maddysin indigestion was her dream when they were in high school.

"I'm not here to make a complaint," she said apologetically. "I'm a high school acquaintance, here to ask her some questions... about... er... the reunion."

The women all breathed a sigh of relief in unison.

"I'll get her," Brandi said. In the process of rushing away from her desk, she knocked the name plate to the floor. H.P. picked it up for her and saw the alternate side read, "Misty."

"You have to share nameplates?"

Tandi's face turned crimson. "My real name is Cassandra. Our name plates always have to rhyme, and today Maddysin chose the 'di' names."

"Ugh. I'm so sorry." H.P. set it back on the desk, with "Brandi" facing outward.

When Brandi returned a few minutes later, she was followed by a stone-faced Maddysin. She was dressed in a turquoise suit with a berry-colored blouse underneath. The boss sure didn't follow the dress code.

"Oh, it's just you! I was worried I'd missed a reunion meeting. Of course, they wouldn't dare make any decisions without the woman funding all the festivities." She rolled her eyes. "Kevin Williams is always trying to cut me out. In any case, I don't have time for social calls. I'm trying to run a business here."

H.P. was going in for the kill, and it would be delicious. "Didn't you sleep with Kevin Williams while you were dating Brad Shumway?" She was using her loudest voice without shouting, hoping it would carry to the furthest.

"And didn't Kevin's girlfriend at the time threaten to jump off the top of the school if you didn't agree to leave her boyfriend alone?"

Maddysin frowned. Or, with her limited eyebrow movement, dipped them slightly. "Follow me."

Feeling triumphant, H.P. waved to the identically dressed women and followed her high school nemesis at a safe distance.

When they'd walked to the end of a long hallway, Maddysin opened two double doors, displaying an impressive shiny, black desk with enormous picture windows behind it.

"Ooh. Nice desk, Mad." H.P. ran her fingers over the smooth surface momentarily, before Maddysin slapped them away.

"Don't touch! That's high gloss black piano lacquer with sycamore inlays, casted bronze ornaments, and Swarovski crystals. I had it imported from Belarus, and it cost me a pretty penny."

H.P. looked both ways through the cavernous space. She couldn't see the end of this place that was bigger than her first two apartments combined. On a fancy hook that probably cost more than her lifetime income, she noticed the leather bag Maddysin carried when she came to the diner.

"I'd ask you to sit, but I know you've got pies to bake, or some other equally pedestrian endeavor."

"That's okay. I get to enjoy the sunshine and breathe in the sea air on my walk back to the diner. If I recall, you came in not so long ago, demanding that I sell to you."

"Oh?" Maddysin's voice rose an octave. "Well, if you came to talk terms, the offer has gone down by ten thousand dollars since the last time we spoke. The world of real estate is crazy, right?"

"Oh, I'm not here to sell my diner. I'm keeping it for now. I'm here to ask you about the last time you and my grandmother spoke. Do you remember when that was?"

"I went to her place weekly, trying to convince her to sell. After a presentation by my developer, where she saw the plans to put a strip mall next door for those who enjoy those types of things," Maddysin paused long enough to roll her eyes. "Your grandmother was gifted a glimpse of the future. All she had to do was sell her property for a nice profit, and turn over all of her original recipes. Do you know what she said?"

H.P. shook her head.

"She told me to take my whoopsie doodle, and by that I can only assume she meant my developer, and hightail it out of her restaurant."

Maddysin had more of a motive to kill Gram Gram

than she'd assumed. "That must've made your blood boil. Nobody blows you off, right?"

Maddysin rolled her eyes in dramatic fashion. "I'm assuming that was all part of her madness, poor woman."

"I spoke with her every evening. She was completely lucid."

"Well, that's not what I heard. Word around town is that your grandmother got into an argument with poor Mr. Thornton and threatened him with a kitchen knife. In the tussle, she slit her own throat."

"The official cause of death was accidental laceration, and Mr. Thornwood wasn't even there."

H.P. felt her cheeks getting hot, and she hated that she'd allowed Maddysin to get the better of her. "I'm... not feeling well, Mad. I could use a little water, if you don't mind."

Maddysin snorted as she rose from her desk. "I'll be back in a minute. Don't touch anything!"

H.P. watched Maddysin disappear before rushing over to the hook, which held her leather bag, and opening it nervously.

In a side pocket, not even hidden, was the letter opener she'd spied on the first day. Using a napkin from the diner, H.P. carefully wrapped it up and stuffed it inside her own bag before returning to her seat.

She couldn't resist more snooping. Maddysin had a fancy, digital calendar on her desk. H.P. picked it up and used her finger to scroll backwards. There weren't many events listed. When she got to February 2nd, the date of Gram Gram's murder, she paused to read the events listed.

"You're so obvious." As if on cue, Maddysin stomped through the office doors, tossing a Blissful Hydration bottle into her unwelcome visitor's lap. "I charge my guests twenty bucks for that, but I'm feeling generous today."

She hadn't noticed that her digital calendar was now on the opposite side of her desk.

The bottle appeared to be tap water with a fancy label, but H.P. opened it and took a sip, just the same. "Thanks, Mad. We were talking about the last time you spoke to my grandmother. Was that the day before she died, or..."

Maddysin sat down at her desk and retrieved a soft cloth from a drawer to wipe the spot H.P. smudged. "It most certainly was not! It was two or three days earlier, whenever that was." She motioned her hand as though she were swatting away a fly.

Leaning forward in her chair, Maddysin grinned wide. "I'm a lot smarter than you think, Feetwater. Since she'd kicked me out, I hired a kid to drop off a flyer. It explained how, as a gesture of good faith and my, let's face it, unparalleled business acumen, I'd ensure customers lined up out the door for the next four months."

"How would you do that?"

Maddysin smiled slyly. "I just acquired an air fresh-ener company. We started production last week in the old Rise 'n' Shine clock factory building by the airport. I was planning on providing a bus each day for the workers to eat at the diner. At a discount, of course."

Gwen mentioned the presence of air freshener ingredients in Gram Gram's body when she died. That, and the bloody letter opener increased the likelihood that the bars of a jail cell were in Maddysin's future. "Did you, perhaps, attach samples of your air freshener to the flyer?"

"How did you know? What did she tell you?"

"Oh, nothing, really. I was just curious. Was it in a bottle, or on one of those annoying smelling strips?"

Maddysin's face expressed a look similar to H.P.'s, the last time she found a moldy cheese sandwich under Dex's bed. "Why are you wasting my valuable time with these insipid questions?"

For a brief moment, they were back in high school. H.P. was wearing her cousin Phyllis's hand-me-downs and her dark hair hung in her eyes. Maddysin walked down the hall with her equally awful friends and kicked H.P.'s leg out from under her, causing all of her books and the private contents of her locker to tumble to the ground simultaneously.

"H.P, you like Brad?"

One of the onlookers picked up his picture from the yearbook, the one she'd covered with goofy hearts. At least Maddysin was too far away to hear. Honeypie Sweetwater didn't want to show her face in Misty Cove again, let alone, the next day, but Gram Gram convinced her that everyone would forget about the incident. Eventually.

"Her home... smelled like air freshener. It was in the coroner's report. It made me curious."

Maddysin folded her manicured fingers together on the desk in front of her. H.P. noticed huge diamonds on both hands. Not worth asking if she married Brad. "Honestly, this is such a waste of time! I knocked on her door the evening after she'd received the flyer, since she hadn't bothered to call the number at the bottom. I handed her more air freshener samples and said I'd be back the following week. And do you know what she told me?"

"Take your stinky perfume and leave?"

"People like me were the melted marshmallow on the bottom of her shoes. She was doing just fine with her regulars and people who saw her billboard on Highway 101."

H.P.'s heart swelled with pride. Her grandmother was the most principled person she'd ever known. "Was that the last time you saw her? No more conversation, like just in passing?"

"If you're asking if she spoke about you, she did." The corners of Maddysin's mouth twitched, as though she were preparing to eat the biggest, juiciest steak. "Your grandmother said you were a colossal failure. Of all her grandchildren, you were the one she least expected to make anything of herself."

And there it was.

Maddysin grinned like a Cheshire cat. "And it appears she was right!"

"Strangely, she left me the diner. How do you suppose that happened if she thought I was such a failure?"

"Think what you like," she sniffed. "I know the real reason she left the diner to you. People talk, you know?"

H.P. swallowed hard. She'd heard so many ridiculous theories already, even from Maddysin. "What did you hear, Mad?"

"Only that your Uncle Sebastian begged her for money and she kicked him out. Their arguments were legendary. Everyone in town knew about them!"

"You're sure? That they were arguing over money?"

Maddysin stood, her thin body towering over H.P. "I've given you far more than the ten minutes promised. You'll see yourself out? Feel free to take a twenty percent-off coupon on the way. You could really benefit from a facial."

"Give those poor women at the check-in a raise. They're shaking in their shoes due to your silly rules, and that can't be good for business."

Maddysin's stony gaze made it evident she hadn't heard one word.

"Thanks for the talk, Mad. It's been... real."

As a parting shot, H.P. ran her fingers slowly and deliberately across the desk, leaving a trail of fingerprints. Applying Mrs. Scheddy's Extra-Thick Crème Lotion before she visited was a good choice.

Chapter Sixteen

Her phone buzzed on her way over to the diner. "Salutations, H.P.! This is Gwen. Mom's bridge partner's uncle died. No autopsy needed, as he'd just won Tony's Tongue Torture Hot Sauce contest. His wife tried to convince him not to eat the leftover peppers, but he felt he had something to prove, since last year's Screaming Trots Virus forced him to drop out a week prior. When he slumped over, nobody would touch him until the hazmat team arrived. The sheriff said they didn't own enough hazmat suits for me to use one, and besides that, everybody—"

"Sorry, I don't mean to be rude," H.P. interjected, though she was enjoying this off-beat conversation. "But why was it that you called? I'm almost at the diner, and I'm sure Edna will be angry that I'm late."

"Oh, right. Mom needs a last-minute bridge partner. A hot body to fill the seat. Ha! Get it? Naughty, Gwen, very naughty."

"No problem. We'll catch up soon. Oh, Gwen? Can I drop off something for analysis? Just for my own clarification."

"Yes! Please do, H.P.!"

A surprise customer awaited her arrival at the diner.

"Dexter Samuel Jenkins! I don't approve of you skipping school!"

Though as a teen, H.P. skipped so often, they called Gram Gram when she actually wrote a note excusing her granddaughter, because they didn't recognize the handwriting.

Dex glanced at his mother briefly before turning back toward the swinging doors. It was only a moment before both his stomach and his eyes were rewarded.

Edna, with a hint of a smile, placed a plate of his favorites—mashed potatoes, chicken strips, and barbecued wings—in front of him. The two of them had formed a bond: the surly old woman and the surly young teen. She was always eager to serve him, because, "your mother probably wants you to eat things she's found on the lawn."

"Kale isn't something you find on the lawn, Edna." After taking a few moments to cool off, H.P. decided to give her son the benefit of the doubt. "What are you doing here, bud? Did I get the calendar confused again? Another holiday I never heard of?"

"Mom, I lost my appetite and couldn't eat lunch, and then I couldn't concentrate in class. I was worried about Dad, so I went to the office and the nurse let me go. She said she couldn't tell if I had a fever or not, but that it was okay to take a mental health day if I needed one. Edna came and picked me up."

H.P. opened her mouth to protest that Edna wasn't his mother, his guardian, or even a friend. But then, she thought better of it. If he were ever truly in trouble, it would be nice to have old Edna to rely on.

H.P. studied her boy's face intently. She wanted to believe him, but he was so masterful at playing her that she never knew quite when he was being truthful. She'd been bugging him to get the mower out of the old shed in the backyard and mow the lawn. It wasn't out of the realm of possibilities that he'd come up with a great excuse to avoid that physical labor.

"I'm sorry I haven't been taking that more seriously. Talk to me about Dad. Any news?"

He scooped a large spoonful of potatoes into his mouth before he spoke. "I called Juliette again. She's really worried about Dad too. She wants you to call her."

"Oh, Dex, I don't think..."

She'd only spoken with her ex's wife twice. Once was the time Dex had his tonsils out. Juliette was very succinct. "Give me the name of the hospital, the attending physician, and his room number. I'll make sure MY husband responds within the hour."

The second time was when Dex came back from a visit, tearful that he'd left his favorite sweatshirt in Florida. "I'd appreciate it if you would send it back, Juliette. He even sleeps with the stupid thing on."

"Oh, not in MY home, Ms. Sweetwater. I have strict rules about nighttime attire. He had to take it off so I could wash it. As I'd assumed, the boy had forgotten all about it, so I disposed of it."

"No!" H.P. gasped in horror. "Juliette! How could you?"

It took much coaxing from both she and Dex to get Eliot to make a trip to the Children's Society Clothing Drop to retrieve it. Even then, Juliette insisted they reimburse her for postage.

"I don't think I'll be much help. Juliette knows your dad better than I do."

Dex paused the conveyor belt of food entering his mouth. "Please? For me?"

She was putty in his hands every time he uttered those words, even if it meant talking to the second least desirable person in her life. At least she'd already gotten Maddysin out of the way. "Okay. But I'll expect something in return."

"What?"

"The next time you need a mental health day, you call me first. Deal?"

"Deal."

"And I would be SOOO happy if I came home tomorrow, and the lawn was mowed."

Dex rolled his eyes. At least she knew the first request would be honored.

The swinging doors to the kitchen opened. "You ready for pie yet? I've got lemon meringue, pecan, and honey. Can't read your pie-o-meter," Basil said playfully.

Dex nodded.

"One of each it is."

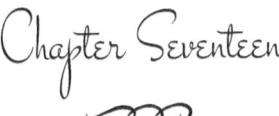

Chapter Seventeen

The letter opener she'd found in Maddysin's purse was now safely in Gwen's hands. Like a dog with a bone, Gwen practically grabbed the plastic bag containing the possible weapon from H.P.'s hands before a proper explanation had been issued.

"It won't take long, I promise!" Gwen sounded like a giddy schoolgirl, not a coroner. "That is, unless there are anymore unexpected deaths."

While she waited for an update, H.P. decided she and Gram Gram needed a heart-to-heart.

H.P. paced back and forth in the walk-in cooler; her arms crossed tightly over each other. Today, she'd found her Uncle Bash's old high school letter jacket in the closet and put it on just for fun.

"Well, I guess I can understand that. You grandkids were always my priority. I would like a recap of what you've found so far, though."

Gram Gram's ghost perched on the top shelf, between a bag of carrots and large jars of pickles.

"Let's start from the beginning. You know I went to see your boyfriend. He creeps me out, quite frankly."

"Lem's a lovely—"

"I know, I know. Everyone thinks the man walks on water." H.P. rolled her eyes. "He had a good reason to kill you, Gram Gram. That man is still in love with his wife, I'm sure of it. Getting you out of the way and absconding with your money so the two of them can live their happily ever after doesn't seem farfetched."

Gram Gram's ghost, though fully formed, usually wasn't detailed enough to show emotion. Today, however, her bottom lip quivered. "You're wrong, Hun Bun. I don't care what you say. He loved me. I can hear him crying at night as he calls out my name."

"Maybe he's calling out your name because he feels guilty."

Gram Gram swooshed up to the ceiling of the cooler, her form now surrounded by multi-colored lights. "Lem loved me!"

"Then why did you want me to talk to him?"

The lightshow around her grandmother's ghost ceased. "You needed to understand my life. You can't solve the crime if you don't understand the victim first."

"What? That's crazy talk. Of course I know you, Gram Gram!"

"Yes, you know the basics, but you have no idea

what made my heart sing. And Lemon Thornwood is one of those songs."

H.P. didn't know where to go with this. Should she feel insulted that Gram didn't trust her enough in life to share her relationship with Lem? Or should she feel comforted that Gram brought them together now?

"All right. Lem made your heart sing."

"And you can't picture the man getting his hands dirty, right? Someone of his financial status would hire the dirty work to be done."

The more she thought about it, the more Gram Gram was correct. "Okay, so maybe he hired your killer?"

"I'm not discussing Lem with you any further, darling."

H.P. cleared her throat. "Moving on, I paid a visit to Maddysin's spa. It's like a cult of robotic women who are afraid to speak out against their leader."

"Kind of expected that. What did she give you?"

"She really wanted your diner. I mean, REALLY wanted it. She said she came in every week to beg you to sell. I guess she finally gave up. Not only did she want to build a big strip mall beside the diner, but she also really wanted your recipes."

"That girl boils my butter churn. When will she grow up?"

H.P. glanced at the ghost with trepidation. "I didn't think she had anything to do with your death, but I've since changed my mind. If she had a connection to the person who drew up your will, it would prove she had a motive to get rid of you."

She hated keeping secrets from a... ghost? Yes, she didn't like keeping secrets from a ghost. That was the space she was occupying now.

H.P. paused to take a deep breath. "Which brings me to my next question."

"No, baby girl. I'm not telling you."

"Gram Gram..."

"I've already made it clear. I'm not entertaining any confabulation regarding my will. I made my decision based on private reasons, and now isn't the time to tell you who wrote it and the contents within. You'll have to make your peace with that."

"Fine. Just fine." H.P. sighed. "You sound just like Edna."

Gram Gram floated around her head and H.P. caught the sweet scent of fresh-baked honey pie. She closed her eyes and took deep breaths.

"You were going to say something else?"

"Huh?" her eyes snapped open. "Gram Gram? Are you still here?"

"Of course, love."

Gram Gram's light shone around her as she hovered above the light. Her afterlife beauty often took H.P.'s breath away. If nothing else, these images would stay with her forever.

"Right. Maddysin mentioned that Uncle Bash threatened to kill you."

"Pish posh. She's got whipped cream between her

ears. Bash never hurt a hair on my head, and we parted on good terms."

"Why would she say that you fought? It was very specific, so I don't think she was lying."

"Couldn't tell you, dear."

"Well, Bash did call me last night. He's coming in tomorrow. He said he needs to talk to me about something important."

"That doesn't sound good. He's had baloney in his bonnet ever since he moved out. Wanting me to fund this or that. I told him he was old enough to fund his own adventures."

If he were going to demand money, there wasn't any to give him. The precious few dollars left were earmarked for the diner.

"Who knows?" H.P. shrugged, not at all convinced her uncle was the villain he was portrayed to be. "I'm going to come in here and clean on Sunday. This walk-in is really a mess."

"NO!"

A cold wind swept through the cooler, pushing H.P. up against the bin of apples.

"YOU'RE NOT TOUCHING ANYTHING!"

It was the same response her grandmother had given every time she'd taken it upon herself to move things around when her grandmother was still alive.

"Gram Gram, even in death, you're impossible."

"Mrs. Jenkins? Hi, it's me, Honeypie Sweetwater."

She'd learned the hard way that her ex's wife expected H.P. to address her formally each and every time they spoke. It was a little power game Juliette played, and as far as game-playing went, she was in the amateur league.

"Yes, Ms. Sweetwater? What did you need?"

"Dex is concerned about his father. He tells me that the two of you were in contact, and—"

"Whatever happens between my stepson and myself is private family business."

Part of her felt good that Dex was finally considered part of her family, and the other part entertained a deep-seated rage. How dare she pretend like Dex was privy to any of their family business?

"I wouldn't be calling you if this were just family business, Juliette. My son is genuinely concerned about his father. Do you have any idea why he isn't answering his phone?"

There was a long pause and H.P. didn't know if Juliette hung up, or just found something better to do. "Hello? Are you still there?"

"Eliot—my husband—tends to disappear. He can be gone for a week or two before we're in contact again. It's completely normal for creative types."

H.P. took a moment to process this information.

"He NEVER did that when we were married. Are you sure that's what's going on?"

"Whatever you're insinuating, Ms. Sweetwater, is completely off base. My husband and I have a wonderful relationship."

"I'm just... concerned."

"There's no need. Eliot will return soon, and I'll make sure he calls your son. Was there anything else?"

"No. Actually... yes."

"What?"

"You deserve better. A man who runs off and leaves his wife and children with no communication isn't worthy of you."

"Goodbye, Ms. Sweetwater."

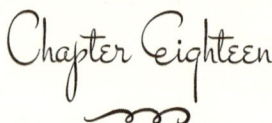

Chapter Eighteen

"El? It's me, H.P. I'm worried about you. Dex says you haven't returned his calls or texted, and for all of your faults, that's just not like you."

H.P. paused, contemplating her next words. "I called Juliette. She's worried, too."

As she hung up, she realized how much anger that would evoke. Eliot Jenkins didn't like his old life and the new one to intersect.

"Did he answer?"

Dex appeared behind her, chewing potato chips in her ear as the crumbs dropped on her shoulder.

"No, baby boy. Juliette thinks he's gone off to nurture his creative side."

She felt silly even repeating it. "I'm positive he'll call you soon. In the meantime, I need to hear all about your speech. I'm so proud of you for making the finals!"

Dex emptied the crumbs from the bag of chips

Chapter Thirty-Four

Upon arriving at her home, or at least her home for today, H.P. kicked off her shoes and tossed her dusty clothes in the hamper before heading into the bathroom. Bash and Dex shared a bathroom and the fact that there were wet towels on the floor in the middle of the day worried her. Uncle Bash wasn't known for his hygiene, that's for sure. His showering before midnight didn't fit the complicated man she knew.

Realizing this was getting her nowhere, H.P. hopped into her own shower and relished a few minutes in the hot water. Back in San Francisco, she'd grown accustomed to timing their showers in order to control a skyrocketing water bill.

Though Gram Gram's account was soon to run dry, she allowed herself the luxury of lengthy, hot showers. The next owner would have to worry about the water bill, as she and her son would be long gone before they had to worry.

Waiting for the water to heat to an almost-hot temperature, she closed her eyes and took deep breaths. Her mind traveled back to the days when she lived here with Gram Gram and a random cousin. They, too. timed their showers in order to allow each child some hot water for bathing. Gram insisted they take turns, but once her back was turned, they would bargain those away for first choice on movie night.

Something disturbing cut short the trip down memory lane. Not a thing, exactly, but a smell. *What was that?* Was it Gram Gram's cake mix dump cookies? It made her feel cared for, whatever it was. H.P. gave herself a virtual pat on the back for conjuring up a scent from her memories and spent another ten minutes in the shower as a reward.

When she finally emerged, all she wanted to do was take a nap before tackling the mess the boys left her. Glancing at Dex's room on the way by, she noticed a clump of covers on his bed. It would only take a few minutes to strip his bed and start the wash. Then, at least, she could close her eyes, knowing she'd done something productive.

While deftly hopping over piles of dirty clothes, she discovered something that made her feel disgusted upon closer inspection. The bed was littered with empty bags of potato chips and cookie crumbs, in some places, thick enough to make little mounds. It was one of her biggest pet peeves, though she'd missed his bedtime entirely and she probably deserved this act of defiance.

into his mouth. At least half of them. The other half would require the use of a vacuum.

"It was all Tildie. She said she knew I was upset about Dad, so she researched whales and how they impact the marine life."

"And you're performing for the entire school on Thursday?"

He stared at her, incredulous. "Mom, no. I told you it's tomorrow, like five times."

"Oh, shoot. Edna is off tomorrow. She's getting new dentures, and she's waited months for her dentist to get back from his tour of Canadian bakeries. Poor girl has quite the crush on the dentist. It's probably better he doesn't know."

"Well, that shouldn't take all day, should it?"

H.P. grinned at her son. "Edna has to show off her new teeth at the retirement center. She's been bragging about them for a month now and they've set up an afternoon party. Of course, she needs the morning to prepare."

The next day, H.P. pushed aside feelings of guilt over missing Dex's presentation, choosing instead to focus her anger on Gram Gram. If only she hadn't involved H.P. in her drama.

Luckily, it was a busy day, so busy, in fact, that she forgot all about the presentation. Without Edna there, all the waitressing fell to Honeypie, at least until the part-timer arrived at noon. Basil even came out to help bus tables in between orders.

When she turned the sign from "Open" to

"Closed," she finally breathed a sigh of relief. Basil appeared with a beer in each hand.

"I think we both deserve this after the day we've had."

"Thanks!"

H.P. chugged the first half of the bottle without stopping. "That went down far too easily. Tell me about you, Basil. All I know is what you told me on my first day. Where did you grow up?"

He took another chug of his beer before setting the empty bottle down on the counter. "I grew up in Seattle, the middle of three. My older brother was a bully, so my baby sister and I stuck together. We even went to college together. To this day, I call her at six p.m. every night."

"That's so sweet. I always wanted a sibling. And your brother? What became of him?"

Basil's face clouded over in a display of emotion H.P. hadn't witnessed from this perennially cheery man before. "He's doing his thing. He studied chemistry, if you can believe it. Now, he's working for a perfume company. I've got to make a stop before I head home, unless you need me?"

"You go. I'll clean up. My son will probably pop a frozen pizza in the oven just to spite me."

It was at that moment that she remembered her only child was doing something entirely out of his comfort zone, and that she had completely blown it off.

She pulled out her phone and dialed his number.

Straight to voicemail. Basil had done so much today, she didn't dare ask him to help with her clean-up, so Dex would have to wait until she finished.

H.P. put on her headphones and listened to her favorite group, Neon Storm as she mopped the floor. It had become a welcome way to decompress after a long day of being nice to customers. As a former back of the house restaurateur, it was exhausting getting used to constantly being "on."

Her second semester, she and Eliot skipped their last class to drive to this concert in Seattle. She told her grandmother that, instead of coming home for her monthly visit, she was spending the night with a friend. This same friend told her mother she was staying with H.P. when she wanted to spend the night with her boyfriend.

H.P. and Eliot drank too much cheap whiskey and ate too much bean dip and instead of driving home as they'd planned, they ended up in a seedy motel, taking turns throwing up.

When the unwelcome sun peeked through the thin curtains, H.P. realized she'd forgotten her birth control device. Maybe Eliot resented her for the quick marriage before Dexter's birth? If so, he'd never told her.

Glancing out the rain-covered window, something caught her eye. A man across the street, wearing a pea-green raincoat stared hard at her.

"Eliot? Is that you?"

Now she really was acting crazy. That's what

happened when she allowed herself to reminisce too long. She squeezed her eyes shut and pictured a beach where she picnicked with Dex. When she opened them again, the stranger was gone.

She scrubbed harder on the black-and-white tiles, as if it would magically erase that night from her mind. When she felt a tap on her back, she whipped around, ready to use her mop as a weapon.

"Ow!"

Tildie's nose spurted blood all over the counter and onto her freshly washed floor.

"Oh, Tildie! I'm so sorry, sweetie!" Rushing behind the counter, narrowly avoiding her own mishap of the wet floor variety, H.P. found a clean rag from underneath the counter and wet it with cold water.

"Tilt your head back," she instructed as she held the towel over Tildie's nose.

Obediently, Tildie tilted her head back, blinking at the harsh lights. When the bleeding slowed, H.P. removed the cloth to survey the damage.

"You might want to get that checked out. It could be broken. I'll cover any cost, of course."

There was no way she had the funds for a mirror, let alone, an X-ray.

"Nice, Mom. Really nice."

Dexter, who had gone unnoticed until now, stormed through the swinging doors and into the kitchen she'd just finished deep cleaning.

"Tildie, what if I give you all the free food you can

eat? Come in here any time and order whatever you want!"

The bell over the door jingled and just as H.P. was taking a breath to say they were closed, the one person she didn't want to see walked in.

"I had to take a call from a client, but if you're offering free food, I'd like to throw my hat into the ring!"

Abe's smile would be temporary, just long enough to assess the situation.

"I'm sorry, Abe. The grill is off and we're closed for—"

"I was just kidding." He moved over to the counter and his expression changed. "What happened, baby? Are those allergies causing problems again?"

"Wait—you're —Tildie's dad?"

Now that she saw the two of them side-by-side, the resemblance was uncanny. Same big, brown eyes and caramel skin, same heart-shaped face.

"Guilty as charged." He turned back to his daughter and gently tilted her chin upward.

His gentle voice and soft touch on his daughter's face made H.P. wish for a moment it would have been her nose that was hit.

"Yeah." She glanced at H.P. for a moment and then back at her father. "All day they've been bugging me. Ms. Sweetwater was nice enough to give me a cold washcloth. I think it's done now."

"We've been working with an allergist in Portland. He says he may have to cauterize the vessels in her nostrils, eventually," Abe continued, examining his unwilling patient as he spoke. Finally, she pushed his hand away.

"No, that's not—"

"Are you gonna whale on Tildie's dad too? Might as well make it a twofer." Dex was smacking his lips with delight. H.P. didn't bother to turn around; she already knew he had a smirk on his face.

"Dexter, don't be rude!" Tildie admonished before turning to Abe. "Daddy, I'm fine. Did you bring the trophy?"

"I feel so bad. We were slammed with two school buses full of hungry high schoolers and I was here by myself. I've just now had time for myself."

Abe and H.P. glanced at the half-drunk beer on the counter simultaneously. Her cheeks burned as she attempted to slide it out of view.

"Ms. Sweetwater, we were voted the best speech in the entire county!"

Tildie had impeccable timing, like that of an adult. She unzipped a pocket in her backpack and pulled out a purple ribbon with the words, "Best Speech, Mrs. Tumble's Class" written in gold lettering down one leg of the two-legged ribbon.

"And a trophy, of course."

Abe placed the oversized trophy on the countertop right beside the half-drunk beer.

"That's so cool!" H.P. marveled. Dex had never actually won a trophy before. When he was nine, his soccer team won first place in a tournament. The team took a group photo with a large trophy sitting on the ground between two boys who'd consumed too much red soda.

The promised individual trophies never arrived and Dex forgot about it, but H.P. never did.

"I'm so proud of you, son..."

When she turned around, he was gone. The only evidence left was a trail of muddy footprints across the once-pristine floor.

"Dexter got one too. He'll probably show you once he cools off."

Abe wiped his daughter's nose with his own pressed handkerchief, even though it looked just fine to H.P. and stretched an arm out. "I realize this is hazardous waste and as such, you may not want to handle it, but I feel, at this point, that you owe me one."

H.P. took the towel and disappeared into the kitchen quickly to avoid them seeing her apple-red cheeks. Tildie's cover story hadn't worked. Now she felt even worse. This day couldn't get worse, could it?

When H.P. returned to the dining area, she carried with her one of the raspberry pies Basil left on the counter to cool. "I owe you more than towel disposal. I've got an almost-teenaged boy. Nothing involving hygiene worries me anymore."

She set the pie on the counter and turned to face Tildie. "Why don't you see if you can find Dex? He's probably in the living room, playing the most offensive video game he can find."

"Is it all right, Daddy? I promise I won't engage in anything that would upset you."

Abe nodded. They both watched as she left the diner and headed next door.

"I don't know how you did it, but that girl is a doggone angel."

"Don't give me too much credit; she's been a genius since the age of two, when she read her first words."

H.P. nodded. Parents bragging about their supposed prodigies were a dime a dozen. "In addition to our freshest pie, can I interest you in something to drink? I've got some rot-gut rum in the back?"

Abe chuckled and shook his head. "Sounds tempting, but I don't drink the hard stuff, although I do enjoy a glass of wine. It started out as a religious thing when I was younger, but it became such a habit, I figured, why ruin a good thing?"

"In addition to bringing your son home, Tildie and I actually came here to invite you both to a celebratory dinner."

"Well, I ruined that, didn't I?" H.P. frowned and turned her back to Abe. "Why don't you take Dex? He's always itching for time away from his mother."

Abe touched the sleeve of her sweater gently; in the same way he'd touched his daughter's face. When H.P. turned toward him, she couldn't bear to look him in the eye. She was so ashamed of the mess she'd made of things today.

"We thought we'd make dinner at our place on

Sunday. I know your diner is closed that day. We'd like both you and your son to join us."

Ghost in the walk-in. Running from the law. Surly teen. She could squeeze it in. "What time?"

"Let's say six."

"I'm so sorry about Tildie's nose. You'll want to get that checked out."

"One thing I've learned about kids, Ms. Sweetwater, is that they're made of rubber."

She knew from experience. "My son certainly is. He's had more close calls than I can count."

"I'll go collect my daughter now. There's a nice piece of salmon calling my name." Abe turned to leave. "Sunday it is."

"Wait! I don't know where you live."

"Dex does."

Chapter Nineteen

She was never sure if Gram Gram liked Uncle Bash or not, or if he was just the only son she had left, so she didn't have a choice.

When he'd appear after one of his mysterious "adventures," Gram Gram treated him to her best breakfast creation, a chocolate chip pancake sandwich with strawberries and cream cheese in the middle, cut into squares.

The nieces and nephews flocked to Uncle Bash, never allowing him to eat in peace until he'd picked up each one of them and told them a funny joke.

When he'd finished eating, Gram Gram shooed the children away. "Go do your chores now. Let your uncle have a confabulation with his mother."

They pretended to climb the worn midnight blue carpeted stairs, but always stopped on the top step, pressing their ears against the rails to hear what came next. The more of Gram Gram's grandbabies were present, the tighter the squeeze, and the more likely their ruse would end in loud arguments instead of inside information.

The children never had to wait long before raised voices and clanging dishes changed the jovial mood of their grandmother's home.

It was better drama than any television show they'd seen, at least the ones Gram Gram knew about.

Rarely would Uncle Bash stay the night. By four o'clock, he'd picked up another one of the keepsakes from his bedroom closet, currently occupied by Pennie, and tromped down the stairs.

The children waited for the sound of the front door slamming behind him before peppering Gram Gram with questions. "What did he want?" "Why are you mad?"

She always answered in the same matter-of-fact voice. "When I want you to know, I'll tell you. Now shoo!"

Maddysin's revelation that Uncle Bash and Gram Gram had many arguments wasn't news. But was it a motive for murder?

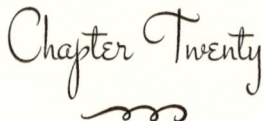

Chapter Twenty

Dex had given her the silent treatment all evening and this morning when she made eggs Florentine and cinnamon toast as an "I'm sorry" breakfast, he only gave them a sniff before leaving.

Knowing Uncle Bash was coming to town made everything better. It may not help with Dex's mood, but it would give her a diversion.

"Does my favorite niece work in this joint?"

H.P. burst through the swinging doors and jumped into the arms of her uncle. Edna clucked her tongue in disgust. "If I didn't know better, I'd think you were raised in the barnyard."

A taller, more jovial version of H.P.'s father, at least the young man she remembered, Bash scooped her up in his thick arms, leaving her legs to swing side-to-side as he hugged her.

The last of the early breakfast crowd stared at them

until Sebastian Sweetwater set his niece on the tile floor.

"What can I get you? Pancakes? Eggs? Waffles? On the house, of course."

H.P. studied his face as she always did, searching for signs of her father. Would they share the same blonde-now-grey hair? Would her father's chin sag, and would he sport a hint of a mustache?

"I'd go for some honey pie, stacked on top of a piece of marionberry, with a dollop of whipped cream on top." He patted his slight midriff.

"My son got your metabolism. You guys are hard to watch when you get into an eating frenzy. And we don't make that anymore. Gram seems to have taken that recipe to her grave, but we do have a nice rhubarb cream. Coffee?"

He reached over the counter and retrieved a cup before setting it on the counter in front of her.

"Give me a minute, and I'll—"

H.P. turned around quickly and narrowly missed smacking head-on into Edna, who had disappeared and reappeared in a matter of seconds.

"There's my gal!"

Bash jumped up and kissed Edna's cheek, taking a heaping plate of pie and whipped cream from her hands.

"Eat your pie, Sebastian. Don't need you starving to death on my watch."

Was that a blush on Edna's cheeks? She returned to the kitchen without further comment.

"I'm the only person she gushes over like that," Uncle Bash bragged as he stuck his fork in the middle of the mountain of whipped cream.

Basil made a brief appearance, probably to see why there was such a ruckus up front. After introductions, Bash furrowed his brow. "Haven't I seen you before?"

Basil chuckled. "People are always telling me I look like their brother or uncle. Usually after a few too many drinks."

"Mom couldn't keep a chef here to save her soul," Bash said under his breath when it was clear Basil was out of hearing distance. He gestured with a thumb toward the kitchen. "Never even met this one."

H.P. turned to her uncle. "What brings you in? You made it sound serious on the phone. I haven't heard from any other family members since we arrived. Kinda thought we were getting the cold shoulder."

Bash temporarily stopped chewing and stared at her, wide-eyed. "Nobody called you? Maybe they're still bent out of shape because you didn't make a showing at the funeral."

The foreclosure, the loss of her job, running from her debts, they hung around her neck like a horse poo. It was surprising that the bank hadn't tracked her down yet; It wasn't like she'd done anything to cover their tracks. "I didn't have the means to drive up. We're only here now, because..."

"Because, what? Eliot paid your way?"

"The man's about ten years behind on child

support, Uncle Bash. What makes you think he'd offer us gas money?"

Ever since the divorce, Bash gave her the impression that he thought their problems were all on her. He was a great fan of Eliot, more so than Eliot was of him.

It was time to change the subject. The last thing she wanted to do was alienate the only living family member still speaking to her. "What do you know about Lem? Gram Gram's boyfriend?"

"Hate him." Bash slurped his coffee.

"Okay. Tell me why."

Bash scooped up the last of his pie, licking the berry juice off his fingers. He shoved an impossibly large bite into his mouth. "You ever hear of Pies, Lies and Alibis?"

"As a game show, or..."

"No, silly. It's a new pie shop that opened up last year. The owner, Cherrie Crumbleton made a big deal of her rivalry with Mom. She was always challenging her to a bake-off."

H.P. frowned. "This is the first I'm hearing of it. Did they ever have a bake-off? And did Gram Gram serve this Cherrie person a juicy slice of humble pie?"

"Mom knew her customers were loyal, so she finally caved in and agreed to the bake-off, with stipulations. She agreed as long as they sold tickets, and the proceeds from those tickets were to benefit Pie it Forward, the charity that gives food and winter clothes to kids in Misty Cove. Mom brought pies to them every week."

H.P. was seven years old when she found herself in front of Pie it Forward. Her thin arms were covered in goose pimples as the cool sea breeze whipped around her.

"Honeypie Sweetwater? What are you doing here?"

She stared at her scuffed Mary Janes and Maddysin's designer sneakers.

"Duh, Maddysin! Funny Feetwater's dad spends all of his money at the Tipsy Turtle, betting on pool games."

At that time in her life, H.P. didn't have the courage to tell Maddysin where to put her observations.

"Charity sounds just like Gram Gram. How much did they raise?"

Bash formed a "zero" with his thumb and index finger. "It was supposed to take place that morning, when Mom was found. They had to give all the money back. That's was Lemon's idea. The man is one of them rich lawyers. Why didn't he just send the money to the charity, anyway? To top that off, all the extra pies went into the trash. Darn shame."

"And Cherrie? Was she questioned by the police?" It was curious that Gram Gram's ghost never mentioned Cherrie, or the imminent contest.

"For what?" Bash guffawed. "Making substandard pastries? They said Mom's death was an accident, remember? Never believed it myself, though."

She felt her insides tighten. "You think Gram Gram..."

"I think it was stress. Mom lost her head when she had too much on her mind. Besides the diner, her reputation was hanging by a thread because of this contest. And then there was the accusation of stolen recipes and Lem Thornwood's having a wife. It doesn't take a rocket scientist to figure out why she wasn't paying attention. That's murder, in my book."

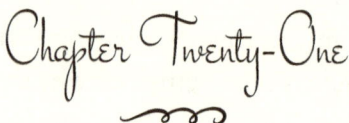

Chapter Twenty-One

"So, just to be clear, you don't believe she was actually murdered?"

Bash's eyes grew wide. "Geez, Honey Bunny, you went dark there! Don't think I ever suggested she was murdered. Just distracted and stressed."

"Sorry, Uncle Bash. You DO believe that Mr. Thornwood's marriage caused Gram Gram to slip and fall with scissors in her hand?"

"Yup. That about sums it up."

H.P. shook her head. Who was she to tell her uncle that his mother was murdered, and that she'd heard it from a ghost? "I still don't know what brings you to town? Last I heard, you took off after Gram Gram's funeral, for parts unknown."

Bash shoved his plate away and used both hands to wipe his face on a single, well-used napkin.

"I'm going to clear a few things out of the attic that Mom wouldn't release. Loved that woman, but she hung onto every memento from all our childhoods. I want to have the chance to throw things away and keep the things that were meaningful."

H.P. nodded sympathetically. "I haven't had the courage to tackle the attic yet. With three daughters, two sons and twenty-two grandkids, she collected a lot over the years."

"I was thinking, maybe Mom tucked away some recipes up there too. Don't s'pose you know anything about that?"

"No, sorry. But you're welcome to search for them."

"Uncle Bash, what do you know about Maddysin Noseinair and her spa?"

"Nothing. I make it a point to stay away from people like her."

"She approached Gram Gram several times about selling the diner to her. Maddysin wanted all of Gram Gram's recipes, too."

Bash lifted his brows and acted as though the thought had never occurred to him. "Did Mom hand those over?"

"No. She kicked both Maddysin and her developer out on their ears." H.P. grinned at her uncle. "Just as we knew she would."

"Mom was predictable, wasn't she?"

"When I visited the spa, one employee told me the business is having financial difficulties, so I don't understand why she would pressure Gram Gram to sell to her. I'm surprised you didn't know."

Bash shrugged. "I wouldn't put it past her. One thing I know for sure, when people die, the nasties come out of the woodwork."

H.P. felt relief that her uncle wasn't there to try and take the diner away from her, or to give her a hard time for her distance from the family.

"Your bedroom is all ready, and you're welcome to stay as long as you like. I do want to warn you, Dex is up at all hours, and he may force you into a game or two."

Bash grinned. "Can't wait!"

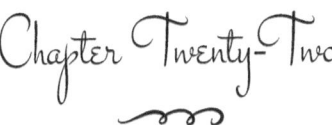

Chapter Twenty-Two

All the way over to Pies and Alibis, H.P. formed a picture in her head of Cherrie Crumbleton: a rival of Gram Gram's, an evil, conniving woman who most certainly caused her grandmother grief instead of what should have been joy in her final days. The Cherrie in her mind was a cartoon villain with dark, arched eyebrows and nails half her body length.

The red-and-white-striped motif of the shop was cute, she admitted to herself reluctantly. Opening the door, a cheery voice sang, "Pies and Al-i-bis welcomes you!"

The woman behind the counter was in her forties. Her hair, held in place by a cherry-patterned headband, was a deep auburn hue and cascaded in loose, bouncy curls just past her shoulders. Her eyes were a striking emerald green, framed by dark lashes and a subtle touch of gold eyeshadow.

When it came to branding, Cherrie Crumbleton

was all in. H.P. studied her wistfully. If only she got enough sleep to look like that. The woman didn't give off the baggy-eyed, long-suffering look that most bakers eventually got.

Cherrie's skin was creamy porcelain in stark contrast to the deep red, ruffled apron she was wearing. In addition to makeup that looked like a professional had applied it, the "cherry on the sundae," her lips, were painted in a classic red, matching her apron and her countertop.

H.P.'s mouth gaped open as she watched this freak of nature floating around her shop. It was almost as though Cherrie were listening to her own songs in her head as she moved rhythmically to the beat.

On the glass counter, there were aprons similar to Cherrie's for sale. She'd covered every angle of marketing.

"What can I do you for?" she asked cheerily. "Wait, don't tell me." She placed a delicate hand in the air. "You don't even have to take the quiz."

"Quiz?"

Cherrie closed her eyes and pointed at an electronic device bolted to the counter. "Take your Pie Q now, and find out which one of our special pies is perfect for you!"

This woman was a genius. A stupid, meanie genius.

"I've got it. You're a Belly Buster Blueberry Blast kind of girl: you've got depth and focus, but you have a secret silly side. With a side of hazelnut brittle ice cream, of course."

H.P. bit her lip. It was growing harder by the minute to keep her jealousy in check. She'd feel a lot better if Cherry Crumbleton bit her nails or cursed incessantly.

"None of the above, thanks."

Cherrie's eyes snapped open. "Are you telling me that for the first time in my entire pie-high career I was wrong?"

"No, your blueberry—whatever—sounds wonderful, but I'm not here for pie." Glancing around, H.P. was relieved the store was empty, though she had a feeling Cherrie's customers were as fiercely loyal as Gram Gram's. "I'm Honeypie Sweetwater's granddaughter."

"Oh?" Cherrie wiped the already-spotless cherry-red countertop. "I thought I'd met all of her granddaughters."

"I haven't been back to Misty Cove for a few years. How long has your shop been open?"

Cherrie raised one eyebrow, as though she were sizing up H.P. for a battle in the alley later. One she would, no doubt, win. "Nine months. It took three years to gather recipes from all the pie-baking princesses in my family. Luckily, one of them passed after I got her recipe."

She giggled like a ten-year-old, bringing a hand to her mouth. Was H.P. expected to join her?

"I guess that is... lucky."

"Oh, gosh. I'm super-duper sorry. Your grandmother just passed away and here I am, making light of Aunt Minnie Mince's death. She was a lovely lady."

"My grandmother?" H.P.'s voice rose, not expecting to hear words of comfort from her rival. "Yes, she was. Or, were you referring to your aunt?"

"Your grandmother, of course, silly billy. Aunt Minnie Mince was a stinker. We were all relieved when we didn't have to listen to her complaints anymore. It was always, 'you did that wrong, dunderhead,' or, 'my feet need oiling,' She had no sense, that one."

"Right. Well, I was told that you and my grandmother had a bake-off scheduled for the day of her death."

Cherrie tilted her head to the side and clucked her tongue. "Sweetie," she began, with what may have been sympathy, or more likely, the lead-up to the sales pitch for another pie, this one perfectly suited for a granddaughter in mourning. "It would be in poor taste to schedule another one so close to your grandmother's death. Besides, I'm not sure Edna's up to the task."

"No," H.P.'s temperature was rising, and when it did, it was easier to get off her game. "I don't want to schedule another bake-off. I'd rather we just give the money to charity and be done with it, but my understanding is that Lem Thornwood gave the ticket money back. I'd like you to tell me why you cancelled the bake-off before it was public knowledge that my grandmother was gone."

Cherrie's face froze. At least, that's what H.P.

assumed had happened when the poor woman couldn't stop smiling.

"Didn't mean to stump you," H.P. replied with just as much snark as she could.

"No, I... it's a small town. Word gets around quicker than butter on a hot Hallelujah Hazelnut Pear pie crust. My relatives around town say the Misty Minds Talk Time page on social media is quicker and more efficient than the newspaper ever was."

"And someone posted on this page that my grandmother was dead?"

Cherrie nodded solemnly. "Your grandmother's long nap was noted. Golly, it makes me want to cry just thinking about it again." She sobbed one very loud, very long sob. Curiously, no tears emerged.

"You visited her the night before the event. What did you say to her?"

"I just wished her luck." Her demeanor returned to the same, irritatingly upbeat version it had been a few moments earlier. "Good luck, and may the gosh-darned best woman win. That kind of stuff."

"Hmm. That's odd."

"Pies and Al-i-Bis welcomes you!"

H.P. turned to see a tall man with thick, black eyebrows standing just inside the door.

"I'll be with you in a moment, Sergei!"

"What was the 'hmm, that's odd' about, Miss Sweetwater?"

"Oh, I heard you threatened her for stealing a recipe."

Cherrie's complexion went from creamy white to blotchy red. "You must've heard wrong. I'm not that kind of naughty-kins. Now, if you'll excuse me..."

She was already looking over H.P.'s shoulder at Sergei. "You can come up to the counter, Sergei." Cherrie glared at H.P. while maintaining a smile on her lips. It was awe-inspiring and creepy at the same time.

"Come try our weekly special next week, Miss Sweetwater! Apple-y-Ever-After has caramel AND chocolate chips with our apples!"

"One more thing, and then I promise, I'll leave."

H.P. grinned as wide as Gram Gram's luxury car from 1972, the one that never fit in the garage. "If you truly had your finger on the pulse of Misty Cove, then you'd know that I'm running the diner now. It's still packed full of loyal customers every day. And guess what? I'm still using her ORIGINAL recipes! Bye now!"

She practically bounced out of Pies and Alibis, with false pride. H.P. only wished she were using Gram Gram's recipes. It wasn't until she was opening her screen door that a sobering thought hit her: if Cherrie lied about why she saw Gram Gram, there had to be a good reason.

As soon as she opened the door, the scent of baking cheese and bread hit her nostrils. "Who's cooking?" she called playfully. "It can't be my Dexie. He refuses to make anything that doesn't come from a frozen bag."

Dex appeared from the kitchen, grinning from ear-to-ear. He was wearing the apron Gram Gram gave to all of her great-grandchildren two Christmases ago: the one that said, "My best recipes."

"Mom! Uncle Bash knows how to make pizza! He worked in a pizza restaurant when he was in college and he made two hundred pizzas every day!"

"I bet he didn't exaggerate that at all."

H.P. removed her shoes and walked into the kitchen, where Bash was placing circles of pepperoni on another pizza. He glanced up from his work when she opened the refrigerator and pulled out a beer. "Want one?" she asked.

"Nope. Don't drink anymore, remember?"

"Oops. Sorry." H.P. stood on her tiptoes and kissed his cheek. "Smells great! I'll leave you two boys to your work while I go through the mail. Call me when it's done?"

He nodded. "Tex-Dex, go turn up your rap music!"

She shook her head as she walked up the stairs. If Dex had made a rap music convert out of her uncle, they were truly meant to be uncle and great-nephew.

Once in her bedroom, she opened her desk drawer and pulled out a lined notebook she'd found in a box labeled, "Honeypie, Senior Year."

On the first page, she'd already written suspects, and underlined it three times. There was a teacher at Misty Cove High who said if you're going to underline a word for emphasis, do it three times, so there's no mistaking what you're trying to say.

He was probably making fun of the notes he found

on the floor after class, where almost every sentence included an all-caps word with multiple underlines, but it stuck.

Underneath "Maddysin" she wrote, "Cherrie." On the other side of the page, she included everything she knew about her relationship with Gram Gram.

Next, she turned on her laptop and searched for Misty Minds Mentions. Thankfully, it was a public page. There were many posts about people in the community, some accurate, others way off.

"I heard there's a new owner of Honeypie's Diner. The owner told me it's going to be a Chinese place by the end of the year."

-sandinmyteeth309

She chuckled as she read through the responses, forgetting for a time her reason for getting on the page to begin with:

"My dentist said it's going to be strictly pizza. Like we need another pizza place!"

-peachykeen911

"It's going to be a new motel. I talked to the contractor yesterday."

-eatmorefish

Finally, she found the post from the day her grandmother died. There were three hundred responses, most of them supportive. It warmed her heart to see.

The post itself read, "It is with a heavy heart that I can report Mrs. Sweetwater is no longer with us. The friendly competition scheduled for today has been cancelled. All donations will be distributed to local charities, as per Mrs. Sweetwater's request. If you wish your donations to be returned, contact Cherrie Crumbleton at Pies and Alibis."

Her heart ached as she thought back to that day three months ago. She'd just had a heated argument with the executive chef, who wanted to use cheaper quality ingredients in order to fund his raise.

Their frequent arguments were the reason she was fired, at least that was what she assumed.

She was in the alley, trying to collect herself when one of her co-workers came outside and handed her the business phone.

"For me? Are you sure?"

The co-worker nodded, twisting the phone in her hand insistently.

H.P. raced through excuses she hadn't given the landlord. I changed banks? My mother has a serious illness and I'm funding the treatment?

"Hello?"

Bash's sobs said more than his words. She'd been dreading this day ever since she moved away. The nightmares that accompanied her move always involved Gram Gram's death. The low-cost counselor she saw said it was most likely guilt over the move and she needed to eat lots of pickles to rid her body of the toxin build-up causing the problem.

Whether it was the pickles, the thought of the new life growing inside her, or her shiny, new marriage, the dreams disappeared.

She scrolled to the top of the page to find the original poster announcing Gram Gram's death:

Anonymous Apron701

She felt a gentle breeze going through the room and smelled the scent of Gram Gram's pies baking and without even turning; she knew.

"Aren't you supposed to be stuck in the walk-in now? Didn't you tell me that? There are rules in the afterlife, right?"

Gram Gram wrinkled her brow and shook her head. "Which whatsadoodle television shows have you been watching? Did you get that from one of Dexter's scary movies?"

"Sorry. What are you doing here?"

"I can see where you're heading with this investigation. You're getting way off track, darling."

"It would have been a great idea to tell me about the bake-off, don't you think?"

"I didn't think it was important. Besides, it never happened."

"Well, you're right about one thing: it is way off-track to suspect Cherrie Crumbleton. That woman has less going on in her head than an empty fishbowl."

H.P. never tired of viewing her grandmother's afterlife form. She was stunning without the worry of paying the bills and taking care of her grandchildren displayed on her face.

"Miss Maddy-kins didn't tell you that she's overextended herself. She's two months away from financial ruin."

She really wanted to feel good about that, especially after her very unpleasant visit to the spa. But the fact that they were both in the same boat financially didn't make Maddysin's impending demise an enjoyable event.

"That's too bad, but it still doesn't explain why killing you would change any of that. If anything, it proves that she couldn't buy the diner."

"Because... because Maddysin knew that the diner had more of value than a building. Underneath—"

"Mom? Mom! Wake up!"

Dex was shaking her shoulders. H.P. looked up at the clock. 7:15 p.m. "I must've fallen asleep."

"Yeah, no kidding! No more late-night TV for you, young lady! We've been calling you for twenty minutes!"

Gram Gram seemed so real. The entire experience seemed real.

"El? It's me, again. I haven't called you this much since I thought you were cheating on me with Hazel Harvest." H.P. paused to chuckle at the memory. "I can't tell you how relieved I was to find out that Hazel had a girlfriend. Anyway, you're not usually off the radar for this long and the boy is worried. Just let him know when you're home safe and sound, 'kay?"

There was a teeny tiny hint of concern in her gut. Not that she cared what happened to the man who dumped her like last week's egg salad. But if something bad really had happened...Dex would be devastated.

"You called Dad again, right? I thought I heard your serious voice."

H.P. turned around so quick, she knocked the one-and-only apple she'd seen her kid eat in a month clean out of his hand. "How is it that you are always around when I'm making phone calls? Don't you have insects to awaken in your bedroom?"

"Ha Ha. Very funny, Mother. Uncle Bash says the messier the room, the more brilliant the mind."

"Good old Uncle Bash," she replied with more than a hint of sarcasm.

"You're worried about him too. I can tell."

H.P. smiled and wrapped her arms around Dex. "It's always been impossible for me to hide my feelings from you."

"We're gonna get through this, Mom. I know Dad is just fine."

Though her heart melted with his words, she experienced a strange feeling of distrust. Was it because Dex had never been so protective before and she didn't know how to handle it? No, it was more that he said it with an eerie calm. Maybe Dex was the one who'd given up on his father?

She was cleaning up after a toddler who like to watch things drop to the floor when Uncle Bash flopped into the booth in front of her.

"You're a sight for sore eyes!" H.P. she said as she

wiped the last of the smashed blueberries from the booth. "What brings you to the diner today?"

Uncle Bash took off his Charming Chucker, Frozen Turkey Throwing Contest 2002 cap and rubbed his forehead. "I'm little upset, I guess you could say."

"And why would I say that?" She left her rag on the table as she sat down in the booth. "Ick! I forgot that's still wet!"

Bash shoved the napkin container over to her side of the booth and allowed her to make a nest of napkins before he continued. "I've been looking all over the place for Mom's secret recipes. I'm hoping you can help. They mean a lot to me, kiddo."

H.P. thought for a minute. "Do you mean the Yokes on You? Or the Fowl Play Fritatta? We don't make those anymore."

His face fell and, for some peculiar reason, H.P. felt defensive. "Those were Gram Gram's recipes and they went to the grave with her."

"Really? When we came back for the funeral, Edna served us up some homemade Block-o-Beef meatloaf, and it tasted just like Mom's."

H.P. nodded sympathetically. "Yeah, Basil felt he should honor Gram Gram and retired her recipes. She had a secret vault somewhere that she kept the originals, anyway. So far, I haven't found it. But I'd be happy to have Basil whip you up an Eggstream Makeover? It's a new dish with an omelet served inside a bell pepper. He's very proud of it."

Bash's dubious stare reminded her that he was a simple man with simple tastes. "What about a good, old-fashioned, three-egg omelet topped with cheddar cheese?"

"That'll do." He slid out of the booth and retrieved a coffee mug and a pot of freshly brewed coffee. "You'll let me know if you come across them, right? Who knows where Mom hid them?"

Chapter Twenty-Three

"I've looked all over the place, and I can't find the recipe you allegedly stole from that awful woman."

H.P. leaned her body against the shelf containing large tubs of butter. "I looked in the recipe safe, and all that's in there is a dirty novel and some moldy cheese. None of your recipes are there."

Gram Gram floated around the walk-in as though she were swimming, first on her front and then on her back. She moved her arms back and forth, mimicking the movements of someone who just learned to swim. She had a look of pure joy on her face.

"I don't know what to say. That's where everything —hold on."

She paused while her translucent figure was perched on the top shelf, where the chocolate syrup sat. "The day before my passing, Edna asked me for the recipe for honey pie. She's been making it for over thirty years, so I thought it was really strange. But, you know, women of a certain age start losing their crocks."

"You mean, 'rocks,' Gram Gram. You convinced me early on that Edna wasn't a murderer. Are you saying now that she's going back on our list?"

"No, I didn't say that at all. Edna's good people. All I said was that she needed a recipe to make a pie. Probably forgot all about putting the recipe box back in the safe."

Not ironically, H.P. had forgotten all about their conversation. Between Eliot's supposed disappearance, the bank's imminent appearance, and running a diner, her mind was completely full.

To top that off, there was an early run on meatloaf sandwiches, meaning they ran out before the lunch rush had even begun. Edna was moving slower than usual, and Basil had called in sick. H.P. searched her mind for one of her favorite recipes at the last place she worked. Quirky Turkey was melted cheese and turkey with a cranberry salsa twist. She'd missed working in the kitchen.

It was two p.m. before she could eat her own lunch.

She heard the heavy shuffling of Edna's feet, and her heart sank.

"Thought I'd take off early today. I've got a date."

H.P. swallowed hard and fast, causing the turkey to lodge firmly in her esophagus. Edna had taken her emergency preparedness course twice, and banged on

H.P.'s back until she spat the food across the counter, narrowly missing the foot of the remaining customer.

"You're either thinking old Edna is past her prime, or that sandwich is worse than I thought it would be. If you'll remember, I told you it was a big mistake. Fried bologna is my backup. Your grandmother ate 'em twice a day in her youth."

There were no pieces of her memory that included fried bologna. "None of the above, Edna. I ate too fast." She took a big gulp of her root beer. "I want to hear everything about your boyfriend. Who is he? Or is it a she? How long have you been dating?"

Edna shot her a dirty look. "You're sure a snoopy thing, aren't you?"

When H.P. didn't reply, she continued, "Remember when I went to the dentist a few weeks past? He said he'd never seen a mouth as pretty as mine before."

It was as hard to keep a straight face as it was the time Dex tried to convince her his class was doing an experiment with bacteria, and he couldn't shower for a week.

"That sounds lovely."

She'd momentarily forgotten why she initiated this conversation. "Edna, can you tell me why there are no recipes in the safe? I was looking for the... potato salad this morning. When I opened the safe, it was gone."

Edna's temporarily serene expression became instantly sour. "Just what are you accusing me of? You think I'd steal from you? From your grandmother?"

"No! Not at all. You're taking this the wrong way, I—"

Edna shuffled around the counter and over to the customer. She slapped his shoulder and remarked, "Can you believe this, Buster? The girl thinks I'd steal from my own best friend."

Buster looked up from his plate, ketchup dripping from his chin, and uttered, "Yup."

"Just forget it." H.P. stood and picked up her plate. "I didn't mean anything by it. I was just curious where all the recipes went."

She went into the kitchen and placed her plate in the sink, gripping the edge of the steel bin. Tears flowed from her eyes, making wet splotches on her plate.

"This is too much for one person. I can't. I just can't."

She could take Dex back to San Francisco. Maybe grovel to one of her old employers and see if they'd hire her again. Edna would have to understand that the bank owned the diner now, and it would give her the freedom to retire with her dentist and live somewhere tropical.

As she sobbed quietly, she heard a muffled voice coming from the walk-in. "What now?" she snapped, throwing the door open so hard that it banged against the wall. "There's nothing left of me, Gram Gram. I'm not the little kid you remember. I'm a big, hot mess."

"Thanks for stating the obvious, Honey. If you had

it all together like your cousins, I wouldn't ask you to solve my murder."

"Why not?" H.P. sniffed.

"Not everyone listens when spirits talk. None, in fact."

"Oh." H.P.'s voice dropped an octave. "I was your last choice."

"Not necessarily. Your cousin, Elvis would staple his head to the table if we let him."

"Great. Elvis the underachiever is one above me."

H.P. regretted her decision to open the door.

"That's not the point. You're here, you're doing a fine job of investigating, and you're going to figure this thing out. Right after you have dinner with that nice-looking man."

H.P.'s eyes grew wide, and she clapped her hand over her mouth.

"Shoot! I forgot all about that! Dex went home with Tildie after school, and I told him I'd close early and join them! He's going to be so mad..."

Slamming the door shut on Gram Gram, she tossed her apron on the counter and rushed through the swinging doors. "Have to leave early, Edna. You close up before your date with the dentist!"

Chapter Twenty-Four

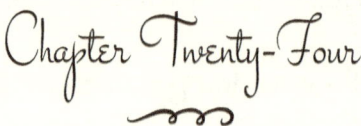

She hadn't even taken the time to look in the rearview mirror on the way over. She didn't dare. A long day at the diner meant her makeup was smeared and her hair drooped over her eyes. It was a given.

Dex wrote down the address for her that morning. As she rang the doorbell, she gave a quick shout out to the universe, "Don't let me embarrass my son!"

The oversized, white door opened, revealing a blue jean-clad Abe. His smile was disarming, and despite recent injuries, he was the most handsome man she'd seen since leaving San Francisco.

"I hope I'm not late. Things got a little crazy at the diner."

He stepped aside and allowed her to cross the threshold of his two-story, Spanish-style home.

"You're right on time. The kids are in the kitchen, making curry. I was given strict instructions to stay away, so would you like to join me in my banishment? I hear there's excellent wine."

"This is the second night in a row that my son has been in the kitchen. I'm a little concerned we've reached the end of the known universe."

Abe chuckled as he poured himself a glass of red wine. "Brought this back from Napa last year. Some of the best I've had. Can I pour you a glass?"

She nodded. "We made a yearly trek to Napa. Usually, I was making food for a festival and Dex would wander around by himself. He loved it."

"And you?"

Abe handed her a glass and sat down opposite her, on a cream-colored leather couch.

"It was a job. I didn't think any further than that."

Abe cleared his throat and moved uncomfortably in his seat. "I'm an overprotective dad, so what I'm about to say is not meant to hurt you."

She tensed. After the day she'd had, there was nothing he could say after that statement that wouldn't end in hurt. "What did Dex do? Did he act inappropriately with your daughter? I've done my best to teach him, but sometimes boys need to hear from another male figure, and his father—"

Abe brought a palm up. "No, he's been a perfect gentleman. In fact, I've told him more than once that I admire his manners."

It was H.P.'s turn to squirm. "Well, what's wrong then?"

"When you moved to town, I didn't know

anything about you. And then, when you came into my law firm, gunning for Lem, well, it gave me cause for concern."

Her cheeks burned with embarrassment. "I let my emotions get the best of me that day. I'm sorry."

"Please listen before offering an apology. You may not feel quite so generous when I'm done."

H.P. took the opportunity to chug her wine. It was slightly sweet and went down way too easy.

"Because I wasn't sure about you, so I ran a background check."

She stood so fast the room began to spin.

"Are you all right?" Abe's arms were around her and she could smell cologne, something with nutmeg. He helped her sit back down.

"I... at least you know. These past three years have been awful."

"Know what?"

She stared at him quizzically. Was he playing some sort of game? "My finances. They're a wreck."

"I didn't uncover any such thing. Just that you'd been fired from your last job for slapping the head chef."

A giggle escaped her mouth. "I did! Jacques Bardot told me that my bearnaise sauce tasted like the droppings from a sick sea gull."

"Well then, I think he had it coming!"

They both laughed so hard, they had tears in their eyes.

"Whatever you two are doing, it's gross." The presence of the two teens had gone unnoticed. "We've got dinner ready."

Dex, while professing disgust, looked happier than she'd seen him in months. Abe stood and offered her his arm. "Shall we?"

She'd never walked with the aid of someone else, but there was always a first. "Sure!"

Abe escorted her into a tiled dining room with a blown glass chandelier, where steaming dishes giving off rich, spicy scents sat on the table.

"My Dexie did this?" H.P. gasped. "When did you go from microwave popcorn to an actual cook?"

Dexter's face burned red, not unlike H.P.'s moments earlier. "There's lots about me you don't know, Mom."

"I don't know about you two, but if I don't start shoveling some of this into my mouth soon, it will turn into an emergency situation."

"Then you'll have to call the..."

Tildie watched her father's face for cues, before they uttered simultaneously, "whambulence."

Mother and son sat silently. Poor Dex. Here he was, worried about his father, and Tildie and Abe acted as though they were best friends.

H.P. picked up the dish closest to her and held it up to her nose. "Mmm. It smells like yellow curry. One of my favorites." She scooped a healthy serving of peppers, onions, zucchini, and chicken in a rich sauce of yellow curry paste and coconut milk onto her plate and realized she hadn't had a chance to finish her late lunch.

"That's right! You worked at Trux Thai. I was there once with a client. We probably bumped into each other that night. It's strange how we pass each other by until just the right time, isn't it?"

As she spooned the frickin' delicious curry into her mouth, she felt a resentment growing inside her. What gave Abe the right to look into her past? Researching a child's parents wasn't a normal way to go about things.

"It's pronounced, 'Truly Thai.' The owner had his own little..." she paused, remembering how handsy Brett had been, as he explained his command of four languages. "...It doesn't matter. It's been closed for over a year. Health department and impatient investors." He probably touched them inappropriately, too.

"Besides, I worked at the back of the house, so I never met customers unless they lodged a complaint." H.P. lowered her chin and her voice. "'Ms. Sweetwater, your presence is requested at the front of the house. Your rice stuck to Mrs. Pickypants' dental work.'"

Tildie and her father were in stitches. Dex allowed a smile to creep over his face.

"Even then," H.P. continued, "we were assigned different nights to pretend to be the head chef on a four-day rotation."

Abe stared at her.

"What?" she snapped with her mouth full of flat bread called naan.

"Nothing. You remind me of someone, that's all."

"Who? Mom?" Tildie asked excitedly. "I thought so too." Tildie turned her body toward Dex. "My mother has a very animated way of speaking. Dad and I have always found it amusing."

H.P. observed a refreshing openness between father and daughter. There was no tension when they spoke of Tildie's mother, only a shared appreciation. If only she and Dex could bridge their differences that way.

"Your mother always required extra room when she knew a good story was coming," Abe remembered.

"Back away, kids. I'm gonna need room," Tildie recited, before all four of them dissolved into laughter.

A loud bell jolted them out of their relaxed trip down memory lane, causing everyone at the table to jump.

"What's that?" Dex asked.

"That's the reminder I set to go off every night on our security system. It's not about security, though. We use it to remind Tildie to finish her homework, and for me to check it." Abe slapped his daughter's back good-naturedly. "Not that she needs any encouragement. I'll let you all in on a little secret. I only check her home-work to give myself an education."

It was already nine p.m. The evening had zipped by. "We need to get home, Dex." H.P. stood and began clearing dishes. When she reached Abe, he grabbed her wrist, sending electricity up her arm. "You do this all day. Please, let me take care of the dishes. I have to do something to feel useful, don't I?"

"At least let me take them to the kitchen. Then I won't feel like a slug all the way home."

Abe shrugged and cocked his head to the side, looking directly at his daughter. "I forgot how tough it is when there are two women in the house. I'm simply putty in their hands."

H.P. stacked all four plates up her arm as she did every day at the diner. When she reached the sink, she felt hot breath on her neck and whipped around so fast, one of the glass plates went flying. It hit the wall opposite her and landed in a million pieces. "Shoot! Where's your broom?"

"I'll get it."

"Why did you sneak up on me, Abe? I don't do well with surprises."

He retrieved his broom from a hidden closet and began sweeping glass chards into a pile. "The other day, when you came to see Lem, I knew you weren't telling the truth."

H.P.'s defenses rose once more. "Is that something you learned from your private detective?"

"No, I..." He shifted his weight from one leg to the other. Abe's discomfort pleased H.P. more than it should.

"I have a good sense about these things. Why were you so upset with him? Did you know him from California?"

There was no way she could trust Abe with Gram Gram's story. "I don't think he treated my grandmother with the respect she deserved."

Her phone buzzed, and she pulled it out of the pocket of her dress.

Got the results from the blood on the letter opener. I took the liberty of running it by my friends at Connect-edFolks.com Bad Gwen! Bad Gwen! I'll bring it to the diner tomorrow after your breakfast rush. G.

Sliding the phone back into her pocket, she frowned and looked up. "Wait, Lem was in California? When?"

"You didn't know?" Abe looked legitimately shocked.

"No. Where was he, and when?"

Abe swallowed hard. "His investment company bought the building you lived in and moved to foreclose immediately on those who were behind in their loan payments."

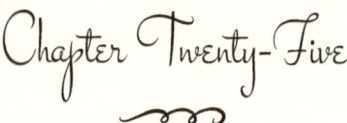

Chapter Twenty-Five

All morning H.P. fretted over Gwen's message. What could it be? She already knew there was air freshener in Gram Gram's system.

H.P. had given up when Gwen didn't arrive by noon. As she rinsed off big pots and pans, she was lost in thought, fantasizing about cooking in that big, fancy kitchen of Abe's. Maybe it was a thank you for a lovely—

She felt a *thunk, thunk, thunk* on her shoulder.

Today, Edna's emotionless face was overshadowed by bright pink lipstick. She looked like a wrinkled version of the holiday doll that used to give Dex nightmares.

"Yes?"

"You have a visitor. I'm not your social secretary."

Immediately, H.P. dropped the heavy pan in the sink and wiped her hands on the nearest cloth of questionable cleanliness.

Gwen was seated in the very last red-and-white booth, sipping on a strawberry shake, and reading messages on her phone. She looked like she didn't have a care in the world.

"Hey, Gwen!"

Gwen looked up from her phone, somehow surprised by H.P.'s appearance. "Oh, hey, H.P. Sorry I couldn't get away sooner. The high school band director brought in band uniforms for their yearly cleaning." She shook her head. "That guy is way too uptight. He wanted to watch as I hung each one on the rotating rack. He said he wanted to make sure I didn't lose one."

H.P. looked around, concerned that sitting with Gwen would make her seem unprofessional to the locals. The last thing she needed was for someone to go gossiping to Cherrie about H.P.'s laziness.

When she realized they were the only two people in the diner, she slid into the booth opposite Gwen. Her arms stuck to the table, and she realized, with disgust, that Edna hadn't cleaned dried ketchup off the table.

"I'll be right back."

H.P. stood, ready to retrieve a rag, when Gwen hollered, "Stop!"

It seemed out of place for both Gwen and a public building.

"Ten seconds. I promise."

"I need to tell you this now, while there's no one else here," Gwen whispered. "It's important!"

Reluctantly, H.P. slid back into the booth, carefully avoiding the sticky spot. "All right, Gwen, you've built this up to be the news of the century. I'm ready."

Gwen slid her strawberry shake to the side and leaned across the table. "Two things, actually. First, I went back over my autopsy notes. I don't know why I was so complacent. It's just not like me. I'm the one who gets things done lickety-split and with so much detail—"

"Gwen!" H.P. snapped, exasperated. "Let's do this while there's no one here, remember?"

"Right. I looked at the alleged scissor wound on your grandmother's neck. It couldn't have been scissors that caused it."

"It doesn't surprise me. What, in your opinion, caused the wound?"

Gwen carefully pulled a folded paper from her pocket and handed it to H.P.

"What is this?"

"Open it."

H.P. unfolded the paper. It was the outline of a woman's body, front and back, just like she'd seen on the nighttime true crime shows. The lawyers always put those on big screens so the coroner could point out exactly what happened. It was her favorite part of the shows, a fact she'd never shared with anyone.

"If you'll look at wound 'A,' you'll see the direction of the wound is right to left, ending near her mandibular—"

"English, please!"

"Her wound went from the top down, not the

bottom up. That tells me that someone was standing over her, instead of the scissors lying underneath her."

H.P. scooted to the edge of the booth, holding her anger inside. "So, you're here to tell me absolutely nothing."

"No, It's not absolutely nothing."

Gwen pulled a clear plastic bag from her pocket containing scissors. She slid it across the table and folded her arms across her chest with satisfaction.

"Are these—"

"Yes, the very scissors Mr. Thornwood said caused your grandmother's demise."

Gwen took a pair of examination gloves out of her pocket and handed them to H.P. "I'd like you to open the bag. We're going to do a little experiment."

H.P.'s eyes widened in horror. "No! I'm not touching the weapon that killed my grandmother!"

"Please, trust me!"

"Reluctantly, H.P. put the gloves on her hands. She heard the door open and turned to find one of the regulars, a farmer who came in frequently, affection-ately nicknamed, "Four Meal Gary," for the frequency of his visits, coming in for his afternoon pie and coffee. "Have a seat, Gary," H.P. called nervously. "Edna will be out soon."

"Fingers crossed she cooperates," H.P. said under her breath. Edna was very adamant that, when she was on her break, she was not to be disturbed. She didn't extend the same courtesy to H.P., however.

Carefully, H.P. opened the bag and pulled the scissors out. She could see flecks of dried blood and it made her sick to her stomach. "Now what?"

"I want you to make me a nice snowflake. You know how to do that, right?"

"Huh? I don't have time for—"

"Just do it. Start by folding the paper and cutting a half-moon out of the middle."

Gwen, Abe, Cherrie, Edna, there was no one in this backwater town with a lick of sense. She set about to make a stupid snowflake, but as she started cutting, she realized something shocking.

"These are dull!"

Gwen smiled and nodded. "They sure are. If your grandmother fell with these scissors in her hand, the only way they could cause a fatal injury is if they punctured her throat. I found no evidence of a puncture wound. Just a clean slice. Now, compare the width of the cut from my autopsy report to—"

"Just tell me, Gwen. I WILL NOT read that."

"The scissors couldn't have been the murder weapon. The wound was too wide to be caused by those scissors. It wasn't Maddysin's letter opener either, as it was too wide. We're looking for a completely different murder weapon."

Dumbfounded, H.P. relaxed against the booth and put one hand on her forehead. "Gram Gram was right. Someone murdered her."

Gwen nodded like she'd just discovered the cure for cancer. "And there is a number two."

"Okay, tell me!"

"I tested the blood on the handle of the letter opener."

"And?"

"And it's from a relative of yours."

"Oh, my goodness! One of my cousins must've killed Gram Gram!" It knocked the wind out of H.P. just thinking about it. But none of her cousins seemed like a killer.

"That's not what I said. The blood came from your family, but the connection is very distant. I'm guessing maybe a great-great-grandparent."

H.P. furrowed her brow. "I'm very confused."

"Did you just say your grandmother told you?"

"Oh, no, that's not what I meant!" H.P. cursed herself for this slip of the tongue. "I just meant that I thought my grandmother—"

"I'm fascinated by the other side," Gwen countered. "I've had a few ghost connections, too. One was an old boyfriend who came to tell me that breaking up with me was the biggest mistake of his life."

"Oh, sweetie. That's just awful!"

Gwen's faraway gaze came back to rest on H.P. "No, I mean, yes, it was awful. But that wasn't why I brought it up. I wanted you to know that no matter what you tell me, I will not freak out and spread the word around town that you're nuts."

For a moment, H.P. contemplated telling her. Gram Gram had never mentioned whether or not it was acceptable to let others know she was still hanging around the diner.

The more she thought about it, the more H.P. decided it wouldn't be wise, at least not now when neither a clear motive nor a killer had been established. Gram Gram's presence in the walk-in would have to remain their secret for now.

"So, you're telling me that Gram Gram was murdered. I'm puzzled, though. The other day when you came in, you mentioned you found air freshener in her system. How do these two things correlate?"

H.P. sized Gwen up. So far, trusting people in Misty Cove was like eating pizza without any toppings: completely useless.

"Please, Honeypie, I promise, I won't tell anyone. I'm a scientist and I relish experiences with no practical explanations."

Gary was clearing his throat on the other end of the diner, more to get her attention than to remove the phlegm. Just as she was about to rise, she heard the loud thudding of Edna's heavy shoes clomping from behind the swinging doors. H.P. was relieved when Edna greeted Gary and they began their usual friendly banter. At least he wasn't upset by the lack of speedy service.

"How's the old gal today?"

"Can't complain."

Oh, she definitely could. Edna spent every free minute detailing her back problems, ill-fitting dentures, swollen big toe and itchy scalp.

H.P. turned her attention back to Gwen. "All right. I'll tell you everything. But you've got to give me your word that no one else will know. I need a secret you have to hold as security."

"I talk to the dead," she uttered, before H.P. barely had the words out of her mouth. "When you spend part of your day with bodies, you have to find a human connection somehow, otherwise, you go completely bonkers."

H.P. opened her mouth to speak, but realized Gwen's revelations were more important.

"I have a colleague who was a real introvert. He died after five years in the biz."

"I'm sorry to hear that."

Gwen nodded. "They found forty-seven blow-up dolls in his home. He'd been suffocated in his sleep by Wendy, Sandra and Libby. He had them labeled." She pursed her lips. "From that day forward, I decided that would not be me. I took my parents up on their offer to run the dry cleaners and became part-time coroner. It suits me well."

"Okay... that's really weird."

"I know. But I don't do anything disrespectful. I'm trying to give them the best sendoff possible."

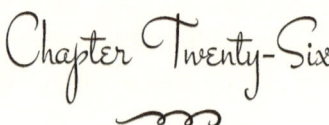

Chapter Twenty-Six

"Uncle Bash wants to take me fishing on spring break!"

Dex and his uncle were seated at the kitchen table, each holding a mostly empty carton of Rocky Road Rising ice cream and a serving spoon.

"Is this what you had for dinner? I thought Uncle Bash was making his famous stir-fry tonight?"

H.P. kicked off her sensible sneakers and flopped down on the recliner. It had been a DAY. Edna left early, again, to meet her dentist for drinks.

"But Edna, you don't drink! What are you really up to? Should I be worried?"

She was half-kidding.

"It's none of your beeswax, Miss Nosy."

Edna took her men's winter parka off the hook and stormed out of the diner without a backwards glance.

"That was weird. Even for her."

Four Meal Gary, having just finished up his regular Wednesday meal of bacon, eggs, sourdough toast and coffee, shook his head. "The old gal's up to something. Mark my words." He brought his coffee cup up to his grizzled face and slurped before slamming the empty cup on the counter. "Wouldn't mind 'nother one."

The very last thing H.P. had time for was another mystery. And where was the evil Ms. Chapel from the bank? It made no sense that she hadn't figured out yet where H.P. and Dex were hiding.

As she was pondering hiding, murder, and air freshener, the bells jingled over the door.

"Ms. Sweetwater?"

"I'll be with you in a minute!" she hollered over the din of the busy diner. "We're one short today."

After she delivered a meatloaf special and a burger with extra cheese and onions, she made her way to the very last booth and pulled out the electronic ordering system Gram Gram installed just months before her death. The one concession she'd made to technology.

"Would you like to hear the specials, or are you one of those smarties who knows what they want before the server shows up?"

"A slice of marionberry and a coffee. Black. And a moment of your time."

She glanced up, for the first time realizing who exactly occupied this booth. Her eyes narrowed. "Lem! How dare you show your face here!"

"I'm afraid we got off on the wrong foot. I'd like to have a few words with you, if it's convenient."

"Does it look like it's convenient?"

H.P. swung her body around, motioning to the full diner.

Lem bent forward and tried to stand. "Right. I apologize. Just cancel my order, if you would, please."

Don't be stupid, Honeypie Chiffon Sweetwater. How many times would Gram Gram's killer come to her doorstep to confess? "Wait!"

"Yes?" There was a note of surprise in his voice.

"I do have a few questions. Let me get your pie and coffee and get the part-timers clocked in early and I'll be right back."

Lem nodded.

What an odd man. He didn't act like a murderer, but did anyone?

When she returned and set the plate overflowing with dark juicy berries inside a pastry and a steaming mug, she sat down across from him.

"Okay, Lem. I'll give you ten minutes of my time. Truth be told, I'm relieved to be off my feet."

The corners of his mouth rose in an attempted smile before he dug into the mountain of pie before him. He closed his eyes as he chewed the first bite. "Mmm. Hasn't lost anything since your grandmother's passing."

"And you're surprised?" She didn't bother telling him that it wasn't Gram Gram's recipe, since those were still MIA.

H.P. slapped the tabletop, causing those customers in the booth closest to them to turn their heads and stare.

"Sorry! I just thought of something funny!"

When they'd gone back to their respective plates, H.P. scowled at Lem. "Every single person who has tasted this pie says it's nothing like Gram's. Every one... but you. Is that because you stole her recipes? Is that why you killed her? Because she wouldn't share them with you?"

Lem's face displayed... nothing. He had absolutely no emotion to show he felt embarrassed, sad, or angry. Instead, he stared at H.P. as though he were waiting for her to say something.

"Well? What do you have to say for yourself?"

"I've never stolen anything in my life. Your grandmother gave me a few recipes, that's true. She asked that I put them somewhere secure. She confessed to me that someone had broken into her safe here in the diner and Honeypie was certain they would break into her home next and hurt her while she was asleep."

"Oh, I get it. You played on her fear of falling asleep while a burglar was in the house. Have you given the recipes to Maddysin?"

H.P. was struck by something even worse. "You're having an AFFAIR with that woman, aren't you? That's why you killed Gram Gram! So, you could spend all your time with Maddysin and help build her business using Gram Gram's recipes!"

"You've got it all wrong, Miss Sweetwater. I loved your grandmother with all of my heart. It's disrespectful to her memory to say otherwise. I thought we'd cleared this up when you came to see me and had to be removed from the premises for your behavior."

H.P. felt her heart pounding as she squeezed her fists in and out. The exercises Gwen gave her were useless.

"Look. I know you killed her. Can we just cut to the chase? Walk me through it, and I promise, I won't tell anyone."

Lem stopped, mid-bite and grinned. "Right. You'll take a confession and just go about your business. I'm not an idiot, Ms. Sweetwater."

"What I meant was," H.P. glanced around the busy diner, where no one was really paying attention to the very dramatic conversation going on in Booth 35.

"What I meant was that once I know who killed Gram Gram, I'm leaving Misty Cove. Dex and I might go down south and live with my Uncle Bash, or maybe up to Seattle. Nothing has been finalized yet."

"You can't sell Honey's diner!" Lem shouted. The din of the restaurant came to a screeching halt as Lem's voice echoed through the room.

"She could have given it to any of her grandchildren, nieces, and nephews, or even to Edna. Instead, she decided to will it to you. Doesn't that mean anything to you?"

H.P.'s heart was beating so loud, she was sure everyone in that room heard it. She began to sweat profusely, something her body usually did under protest, like when she'd been working the weekend dinner hour in Thrush and everyone else was dripping while she barely had a few beads on her forehead.

She'd taken to splashing copious amounts of water on her face in the bathroom, so no one would question her work ethic. Today, however, the opposite was true.

"I don't know why! Can't you see? The 'why' of her death, my ownership, and my life. None of them make any sense!"

Lem's face was fuzzy. Was she dreaming? That would make sense. She'd been having lots of dreams about work and none of them went well.

"I'll just take that pie out of your way, if you're not going to enjoy—"

She understood her body was falling. Whether it was forward, backward, or through space, she couldn't be sure.

"Is there a doctor here?"

Everything went dark.

Chapter Twenty-Seven

When she opened her eyes again, it wasn't the sterile room that jarred her senses. It was the person seated beside her bed.

"You gave us a little scare, H.P."

Gwen stood and smoothed the covers. "I've waited this long to make a friend. It figures she would find her way to my autopsy table before we had a chance for a movie and popcorn night. Bad Gwen. Bad Gwen."

H.P. blinked again and again, trying to process what was happening. "Am I... dead?"

There was a harsh knock on the door as Bash and Dex entered her hospital room. Dex rushed to his mother's side, hitting the bed so hard, it jolted H.P.'s I.V. in her arm, causing a sudden rush of pain up the back of her hand and into her shoulder.

"Ouch! Careful, bud!" She kissed the top of his head, already regretting her words. He must have been scared out of his mind.

"Mom, Tildie's dad came to school and pulled me out of class." Dex was talking in muffled sounds into her hospital gown. "He said you were sick and that I should go to the hospital with him."

"I'm still unclear. What happened?" H.P.'s eyes darted from Gwen to Bash and then back to Gwen. She was the medical professional, after all.

Gwen cleared her throat as though she were about to make a presentation for other coroners about a body found in unusual circumstances.

"Vasovagal syncope. You passed out because your blood pressure is in the stratosphere and when you bent over to yank Lem's pie away, it dropped like a fifty-pound weight."

"I was so scared!" Dex cried into her gown.

Even though he wore a mask of middle school bravado most of the time, there were still glimpses of a vulnerable little boy inside. "I know, I know," H.P. whispered. "It's going to be okay, darling."

"Can I have a few minutes alone with my niece?" Bash had the same look on his face that he did when he was about to punish her for going through his underwear drawer. It held such naughty prizes as cigarettes, aspirin, gum and naked pictures of women, those with bodies H.P. didn't believe were real.

"I've got a twenty-dollar-bill burning a hole in my pocket, kid. Let's go raid the vending machine!"

Gwen held out her arm and, surprisingly, Dex slid off the bed and followed her.

"He doesn't even know Gwen! My boy is shy

around adults, isn't he? Maybe I've been out longer than I thought. What year is it?"

Bash guffawed, as he always did when he thought something was funny, even though everyone else in the room didn't. "When you fell over, you landed in the pie, causing the plate to break and give you quite the gusher."

She immediately brought a hand to her forehead, which hurt the moment she touched it. "Stitches?"

"Seven. I still have the family record, though." Bash said proudly. "Survived the needle eighteen times. The doc said he didn't know how that buzz saw didn't shear it clean off."

"A cut on my forehead wouldn't make me pass out."

Bash looked up, disrupted from his strangely happy memory. "No, it was your blood pressure. The doc says you're going to need some meds and less stress."

It was her turn to chuckle at something completely absurd. "I have a teenager, a business to run, and a murder to solve—"

"What murder? And why is it up to you to solve it? Are you moonlighting for the police?"

His accusatory tone was totally out of character for her soft-hearted uncle.

"I just have some questions about Gram Gram's death. The whole thing is weird, isn't it?"

Bash shrugged. "I dunno. Mom was always having crazy accidents. Do you remember the time she ate too many pickles and ended up in the emergency room with severe heartburn?"

H.P. nodded. "This is different, Bash. Something's up. I can sense it."

"Care if I change the subject for a minute?"

She attempted to push herself up in bed, avoiding too much movement from the arm with an I.V. needle in it and looking straight ahead so that her forehead didn't throb again.

"Sure."

Bash sat carefully beside her, resting one of his huge hands on her knee.

"I didn't come back to get stuff from my room. I'm here for Mom's recipes. I've looked everywhere and I can't find them. You know I helped start the diner and I feel like I'm entitled to the originals."

He wasn't there to see her at all. "Why didn't you just tell me in the first place? I would've helped you look for them. I don't know where they are, unfortunately."

"Dex helped me tear the place apart, and all we came up with was a coin from the second World War and Mom's favorite earrings. It was pretty cool that his favorite uncle got him out of the last two classes of the day."

H.P. was both shocked and offended. The fact that he was involving her son in his deception was hurtful on its own, but instructing her boy to tear the place apart made her already churning stomach turn.

"Dex isn't supposed to go with anyone unless I've

arranged with the school ahead of time. Please don't do that again, Bash. I'm already in hot water with the staff. I'm supposed to initial all of his homework to prove he did it and it's easy to forget."

"You're right, Honey Bunny. It won't happen again, I promise." He reached over and kissed her forehead. "I'm gonna go now. The doc said he'd be back around to check on you and explain your new meds."

"Did you say, 'meds'? Just how many do I have to take?"

"He wouldn't tell me. You're spending the night in this lovely establishment, and we'll bring you home tomorrow."

Bash paused and slapped the doorway. "H.P., don't worry about Mom. Whatever happened, she's gone now and nothing you do will bring her back. I know you loved her. Let her rest in peace."

The quiet after he was gone was harder than the words he spoke. He was right, though. It was ludicrous: trying to find a killer in a town that didn't reveal secrets was a losing matter. And who would have killed her? Lem? He insisted he wouldn't.

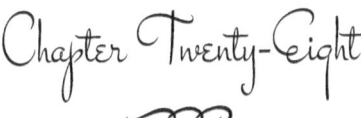

Chapter Twenty-Eight

She hadn't been in the walk-in for two weeks. Whenever they needed something, she'd find an excuse for Edna to retrieve it. Her excuse was always that she was feeble after her hospital stay.

"Edna, could you get the mayonnaise? It's on the top shelf, and the doctor said not to reach up high. You know, because of the I.V."

Edna grumbled, but eventually shuffled into the walk-in.

"Edna? Could you get the lettuce? That bag is very heavy, and my shoulder is still sore, you know, from the fall."

It wouldn't last forever. H.P. would have to come up with a permanent reason to stay away. Either that, or the other, less appealing option.

"I was so excited when you called!"

Gwen slid into a booth, her pants squeaking as

they moved across the vinyl. "Are you feeling better? I'm surprised you have the doctor's okay to come back so soon."

Given the doctor's dire warning, "Change your ways, or next time, you'll be enjoying our company for a much longer stay," she chose to carefully avoid answering that question. "I never had a chance to thank you for hanging out with my son while I was in the hospital."

"He's a great kid. I'd hang with him any time. And he probably told you how I went on and on about my parents." Gwen rolled her eyes. "Yeah, that's how I scare people away."

"He didn't mention anything. He's very good at keeping secrets."

There was a thumping sound against the window. Cinnie was rubbing back and forth against the pane. Without even leaning forward, H.P. could hear the rumble of her purrs.

"Shoot, I must've left the door open. We've been trying to keep her inside."

No matter how cold, or how lonely, this sweet kitty always purred like her life was perfect.

H.P. slid a decaf, oat milk, two pumps of caramel and a half-pump sugar-free chocolate latte in front of her friend. "You mentioned that you had an interest in the afterlife?"

"You too? I knew there was another reason we connected!"

Gwen retrieved her phone, jiggling her shoulders back and forth in excitement. "I'm in eight online ghost hunter groups, mysteryvangwen44. What do you want to know, and I'll post a question!"

It took everything in H.P. not to laugh. Her forehead still hurt, so that was a big incentive. But Gwen's demeanor was almost... cute. "I believe we have a ghost here, in the diner."

"Really?" Her voice rose two octaves. "Can I talk to them? I've got an EVP recorder, an EMF recorder and flashing lights that I can borrow from our local ghost hunter group too."

Gwen reminded H.P. of Cinnie, when she paced back and forth eagerly at the window, hoping some scraps were coming her way. Always eager and upbeat.

"I have no idea what any of those letters mean. I was thinking more along the lines of a séance or something. I want this ghost to leave, but I don't want to force them out in a mean way. More of a gentle shove to the afterlife."

"Pssht."

Gwen pushed the air with her hand. "Those are for amateurs. I can track your ghost by scientific means! I'm a founding member of Here for the Boos. Six of us track ghosts every third Wednesday, so I've got experience.

When we make contact, I'll make sure this fella gets the message that he's not wanted around here."

"But you won't... hurt... the ghost?" H.P. was

suddenly feeling very protective. Dead or alive, this was her Gram Gram.

Gwen giggled in the voice of an embarrassed teen girl. "Oh, you're silly. There's no way for us to hurt the dead. They're more of an idea, like the way we think of a cloud. They're puffy and fluffy and we imagine how they'd feel if we could lie on them and take a nap. You can see them, you can think you know exactly how they'd feel to touch, but in reality, clouds are just minute water droplets and ghosts are just air."

H.P. frowned. "So, you're saying that my ghost is just a product of my imagination?" She slid over to the edge of the bench, ready to make a smooth exit. "I should have known better than to trust anyone with this information. Enjoy your food."

"No! Wait!" Gwen pleaded. "I was simply giving you an example. It has no bearing on how I feel about ghosts. I wouldn't have maxed out my credit card if I thought it was a bogus operation."

She took a moment to size up Gwen.

The whole reason she and Dex came to town was to find Gram Gram's killer. Now, she was asking someone to use her fancy gadgets to rid the diner of Gram Gram once and for all. H.P. was no closer to finding the killer either.

"You know what? I've changed my mind. I've decided I like having this ghost around. It kinda adds character, don't you think?"

Gwen's face fell. "Oh. I'll respect your wishes, then."

She'd really stepped in the mud. Honeypie Sweetwater's intention was never to make enemies. Brock Lee, the executive chef at The Snooty Fork was one exception. Though she never understood what she'd done to become the subject of his wrath, once he made his intentions clear, she came at him with all of her force.

"Let's compromise. I'll let you in after-hours to record my ghost as long as you don't try to scare it away. Do we have a deal?"

She slid her slender hand across the table expectantly.

"Look, if this is going to cause issues, I—"

"I've got a full diner. I wouldn't propose this deal if I didn't mean it."

"Okay." Gwen placed her small, sweaty hand in H.P.'s. "I'll be here at seven tomorrow night. And I wouldn't mind another piece of this pie."

"Deal."

H.P. stood and straightened her apron. "Do you know anything about our little purr machine out there?" She turned her body toward the window as Cinnie arched her back and rubbed the window for the millionth time.

"Dex insisted we adopt her, but if she belongs to someone else, I'd like to make sure she gets home."

Cinnamon Biscuit Maker had already won their hearts. She slept, curled up in Dex's bed every night, and Uncle Bash sang to her when he thought no one was listening.

"If I remember correctly, her mother was a casualty of the highway. Someone just passing through saved the kitten. I don't know why she ended up as a stray."

H.P. breathed a sigh of relief. "She's not a stray anymore."

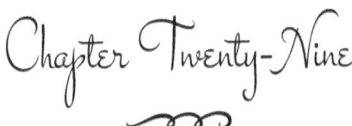

Chapter Twenty-Nine

Gram Gram's backyard shed was something of a childhood legend.

Her grandmother professed to be a gardener at heart, purchasing gardening tools and seeds. But when the time came to actually plant, she'd be far too busy with the diner. Year after year, the shed filled with supplies until one day, she asked the grandchildren to clean it out. As a reward, they could use it as a playhouse.

Being a bit of a garden supplies hoarder, all of her grandchildren lost interest before completing the task.

When H.P. was five, she and a cousin decided to make the shed their "vacation home." They put on their swimsuits and sunglasses and brought bathroom towels to sit on.

Once the other cousins found out, they hid in the shed to scare the girls each and every time they decided to play vacation. It got so bad that H.P. had nightmares, and Gram Gram forbade her from entering ever again.

This gave the older cousins a perfect opportunity to make up stories about various occupants of the shed, the "real" reason H.P. wasn't allowed to enter.

One summer, the biggest instigator of trouble, Cousin Brillo, made up a new form of freeze tag. In its original form, one person was "it."

When the game began, the person who was "it" chased everyone else. When the player who was "it" tagged another player, they tapped them and said "FREEZE!" The kids who weren't "it" ran around Gram Gram's yard like crazy, staying out of reach of the "it" person.

In Cousin Brillo's version, the "it" person lost the game when they failed to tag the other cousins within his time frame. Cousin Brillo received a fancy Chimex watch for Christmas that year and he was always finding a reason to time things. He banged on the bathroom door if a cousin was spending longer than the allotted two minutes inside.

The losing player was forced to spend five minutes in the dark shed, supposedly with their eyes open. When they emerged, Cousin Brillo would quiz them on the shed's contents, just to make sure they didn't cheat. Conveniently, he never lost.

Everyone else remained terrified to enter, because Boogerman, Dark Dagster, Deader Than Dead Dora, or No Eyes Nan, each with their own terrifying story of gore and child torture, might attack.

Three cousins wet their pants, and another refused to talk for a month. Thankfully, someone told on Cousin Brillo. That should have been the end of it, but the last time H.P. spoke to some of her cousins, they were still spending time on a therapist's couch, thanks to Cousin Brillo.

It was for this silly reason that H.P. avoided the shed to this day. Gwen requested very specific things for her in the diner: an extension cord, four feet long, two high-powered flashlights, a hammer, and some gardening gloves. H.P. remembered seeing all the items on one of her memorable trips to the shed.

"Don't cry, or the ghost will chop your head off," Cousin Brillo instructed as a smile crept across his freckled face.

For a moment, she thought about waiting until Uncle Bash and Dex returned from the grocery store. They wanted to make a stir-fry for dinner and vegetable consumption was high on her list for her son.

"Stop being such a baby, Honeypie Chiffon Sweetwater. You're a big girl who's raised a kid on her own and moved to another state under the cover of darkness. There's nothing in there but some cobwebs and a few friendly spiders."

She grabbed the door handle and turned it slowly. Using her phone, she examined the rotted wood ceiling and extensive cobweb patterns before stepping inside. Nothing she hadn't expected. It took a few minutes to find the string for the pull light. Now that she was an adult, reaching for the string wasn't the scary proposition it was in her childhood. No ghost would get her before she turned on the light today. She yanked on the string several times and finally came to the conclusion that the bulb was burned out.

Setting about her work, she found the wooden work bench her grandfather had lovingly crafted for his wife on their twentieth wedding anniversary. Gram Gram told the story often of how she'd been expecting the pretty necklace she often pointed out in Shiny's Jewelry Store window. She'd even cut out an ad from the newspaper, circling the necklace and underlining the price three times.

H.P. slowly made her way through the rusted tools, fearing she would end up with glass stuck in the bottom of her worn shoes. As she shone the light on the ground, she had the feeling she was being watched.

"Stay on task, Sweetwater. There's nothing here but your wild imagination."

It only took a few minutes to find the items on her list and when she'd finished, she beamed her light around the shed. There was absolutely nothing there. No ghosts, no spiders, not even an errant squirrel.

When she returned to the house, she stripped off her uniform and jumped into the shower. There was no sense in bringing cobwebs into the diner.

As she dried her hair with her hairdryer, her mind drifted. The bank hadn't found her yet, for whatever reason. She almost felt sorry for old Sistene. The poor woman must have lost her job by now. Some day when

Dex was out of college and living the successful life he was owed, she would tell him the story of their escape and why she had to pull him away from his friends so suddenly.

H.P. paused to look in the mirror. The dark circles that had taken up residence under her eyes were dissipating. It was funny when she thought about it: life on the run, worrying about a ghost, and a skeezy lawyer must have been agreeing with her.

She took the brush and went one more round with the blow dryer.

"You're giving up too soon, sweetie."

H.P.'s head snapped around. "Gram Gram? Are you here? I didn't think you could leave the walk-in!"

There was no one in the bathroom with her. She remembered the first night they'd spent in Gram Gram's home, how odd and yet still comforting it was to see her ghost. When she'd fallen asleep at her desk, Gram was in her dreams. Whatever strange rules her grandmother's ghost was living by, they seemed to change by the day.

"You came to find my killer. Don't give up until you do. I have faith in you, my girl. It's perfectly fine to ask for help. I'm sure there are others with the resources to help you."

A shiver went up H.P.'s spine. The shed had nothing on Gram Gram's master bath. H.P. hurriedly dressed and left the bathroom.

Dex and Uncle Bash were chopping vegetables and telling corny jokes in the kitchen.

"Oh, hi, Mom. We were wondering where you got all of those supplies?"

Dex took his knife and pointed it wildly at the pile of equipment she'd dropped at the back door, narrowly missing her nose.

"Oh, my friend, Gwen has a little adventure planned. Luckily, we had everything she needed in the shed."

Both Bash and Dex turned a color of white she called "school paste."

"Was it something I said? Don't tell me you're both afraid of that thing too! It needs a new lightbulb and probably some roof repair, but it's a good structure."

"I've told the kid how much that used to scare you," Bash finally uttered. "A little fear never hurt nobody though."

"Yeah. He told me all about your backyard games," Dex added quickly. "They sounded stupid to me."

H.P. slid onto a stool, where she began putting her shoes on. "That's because you aren't a six-year-old who was scared of her own shadow. That place was terrifying. I had flashbacks today; I was sure the Ghost of Mrs. Hauntwell was breathing down my neck." She giggled, hoping they would laugh too.

Both men returned to their duties, hurting her feelings just a little. "I've got to go back to the diner tonight, but I won't be long. Uncle Bash, will you make sure my brave young man finishes his homework?"

Bash nodded.

"Oh, Mom, you'll never guess who I saw today at Mr. Bunce's office?"

"I'm going to guess... the president!"

She smiled, remembering Abe's first introduction.

"No, that's dumb. We saw Edna! She was in Mr. Thornwood's office and then when she realized we were watching, she got up and moved the coat rack in front of the window."

"Maybe she needed some legal advice?"

Dex shook his head. "They came out right before Tildie and me went home. Mr. Thornwood goes, 'see you next week, Edna.' Do you know why?"

She yanked her pants over her shoe and looked up. "Can't say as I do, bud."

"Mom, do you know what happened to the man who lost his left arm?"

It always amazed her how quickly her son could change gears. "No?"

"He's all right now."

Dexter looked at his uncle and the two men erupted in laughter. It felt good to hear that.

After a delicious supper of stir-fried chicken, peppers, onions, snow peas, cherry tomatoes and Bash's Secret Sauce over rice, she found her coat. This was the family dinner she'd dreamt of when she and Eliot married, and here she was, bowing out early, she mused.

"I won't be late." She kissed her son on the head and waved to Bash.

"Let's talk when you get home," he called from across the room.

She was beginning to enjoy these late-night chats. Bash would mix up his famous Bashed Hot Chocolate, a combination of powdered chocolate, milk, tequila and cinnamon. It was his signature drink, one that each grandchild tried to convince the grownups they could try.

The two of them sat on Gram Gram's favorite brown leather couch sipping their drinks while reminiscing with family stories. "Do you remember when Meredith thought it would be funny to leave a puddle of lotion by my bed? I got up the next morning and fell forward, right into the hundred dollar stereo I'd saved up to buy from Trembles Department store."

Bash chuckled uneasily. "All your cousins laughed, but it was more about their relief they hadn't been the focus of her pranks instead of making fun of you."

H.P. nodded. "You're probably right. At the time, making a trip to the E.R. to remove remnants of my stereo from my ears was secondary to the betrayal I felt."

Pushing both that memory and their recent memory from her mind, H.P. drove to the diner. It was both humiliating and humorous that she let her fear get the better of her, but she was a grownup and if she wanted to drive 800 feet, she was entitled to do so.

H.P. waited in the parking lot for Gwen. "How old do you have to be to get rid of your fear of the dark, Sweetwater?"

She adjusted her rearview mirror, remembering she hadn't checked her teeth for evidence of Uncle Bash's delicious meal before leaving the house. As she picked at her teeth, she noticed a silhouette behind her.

Her self-defense classes kicked in as H.P. removed the keys from the ignition and positioned the largest key between her first and second fingers. It made for a quick "poke 'em in the eye" weapon.

"Who's there?" she shouted as she whipped around, the key protruding from between her second and third knuckles.

Don't quit now. You need a friend.

"Gram Gram? How did you get—"

When she heard a knock on her window, she jumped so high, her head hit the ceiling of the car. H.P. leaned against the headrest, trying to catch her breath.

Gwen knocked again, this time, leaning so close that her breath left a delicate circle of fog in front of her.

H.P. opened the door and narrowly missed hitting Gwen. "Sorry! I was lost in my thoughts. Are you ready?"

Gwen's eyes showed doubt, but she nodded. "I've got all of my equipment in my trunk. Will you help me carry it inside?"

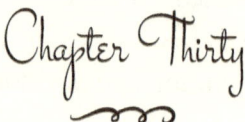

Chapter Thirty

Gwen sat at a rickety table H.P. found for the occasion, dressed as though she were planning an arctic expedition.

"I'm impressed, Gwen. You've invested a lot into this hobby!"

Clad in a heavy jacket with thermal gloves, she was dressed for a duel with the elements and the ethereal, H.P. mused.

Gwen turned abruptly, causing the folding chair to squeak in protest. "This isn't a hobby, H.P. Hunting ghosts is a serious business. These are people's loved ones who, for whatever reason, can't leave our world behind!!"

"Sorry. I didn't mean to offend you, Gwen. Can you show me what some of this stuff does?"

Around her neck hung a black box. She pointed to what looked like a small antenna on top. "This is an

EMF meter, which measures any changes in electromagnetic activity in the cooler. The reading on the screen will change dramatically when an entity is present."

Surrounding the screen was an array of LED lights ranging from green to red.

"These will light up different colors, alerting us to the entities' presence."

"You must've spent a lot of time learning how to use all of this equipment!" H.P. still wasn't convinced this was more than a way to squeeze money out of suckers.

"These are the other tools of the trade: a digital voice recorder for capturing spectral whispers; a thermal camera to detect any apparitions present; and a spirit box to convert radio waves into a medium for otherworldly communication."

It took over an hour to set up Gwen's beeping and buzzing electronics. Gwen tested them all for sound and then sat down on the rickety folding chair H.P. found in the storage area.

"That's all you need, then?"

Gwen's shoulder's dropped. "You're not staying?" Her voice bordered on whiney, but H.P. chose to think of it as sad instead.

"No, this is your project. I thought I'd deep clean the prep area while you're working. That won't bother you, will it?" H.P. felt a pang of guilt. She was pawning her grandmother off on a practical stranger.

Gwen shrugged, clearly upset. The two women,

stared at the ground, neither speaking for several minutes.

"Tell you what; let's leave the door to the walk-in open. Electric bill be damned! I can hear what's going on and I'll be right here if you need me."

Gwen's face brightened. "That's the perfect solution, H.P.! Oh, you'll hear me talking. I record all of my sessions; in case I want to review them later."

As Gwen settled in with her equipment, H.P. removed all the utensils from the prep area. She pulled her ear pods from the pocket of her jacket, but then changed her mind. If Gram Gram's ghost had something to tell a stranger about her killer, it was important to hear it.

"Great, I forgot my sweater," Gwen muttered to herself, rubbing her arms in a futile attempt to generate warmth. H.P. chuckled softly. You'd think a woman who worked with dead people would be used to the cold.

"I've got several, Gwen."

H.P. disappeared, returning momentarily with Uncle Bash's letter jacket. Though Gwen seemed hesitant, she slipped it over her shoulders, allowing the coat to swallow her completely.

"Oh, I almost forgot. Is there a name in your head? Something or someone that's been on your mind lately? If I can call them by their name it makes them feel more comfortable."

H.P. swallowed hard. "Nope. None at all."

"That's fine, just fine. I can chat with anyone."

"Do they speak often?"

"It depends. If they have something important to tell us, then yes. Some of them don't have enough energy for more than one word, and that's frustrating for both of us. I'll need you to be as quiet as a mouse while I set a baseline."

H.P. nodded.

"All righty. Gwendolyn B. Folds, aka, @mystery-vangwen44, aka, ghostgrabbr909, aka, hear-ingvoices34..."

She turned to face H.P. before whispering, "I have to give all of my social media names, just in case something happens to me."

The chair squeaked as she pivoted back. "...Here, in the walk-in cooler at Honeypie's Diner, " she continued. "It's a rainy Tuesday evening, temperature is 46, humidity at 90 percent and the feel of the evening is... mysteriously soupy. Only two of us are on site. Owner reports possible spectral sightings. Surrounded by the regimented ranks of vegetables and dangling meats, the space is more than a storage area—it's very possibly a threshold into the unknown."

H.P. suppressed a giggle.

"Now, I'll attempt to contact the spirit form in the cooler. I'm here, waiting for you. I'm not afraid of ghosts. You can tell me anything."

The only sound came from the sink, where a faucet dripped water rhythmically.

"Mrs. Sweetwater, are you here with us?" she asked, her voice steady but friendly. The digital voice recorder's red light blinked in the dim light, standing sentinel on a crate of frozen mixed vegetables.

All of a sudden, H.P. didn't want Gwen speaking to Gram Gram. This was a poorly thought-out plan, like most of hers were. "How do you know it's my grandmother?" H.P. hissed. "Ask if it's someone else!"

Gwen furrowed her brow and shook her head.

The EMF meter, hanging from a strap around her neck, was quiet. No flickering lights, no erratic beeping —yet. Gwen wasn't deterred. "Spirits are like cats," she whispered, "curious yet cautious, and often take their sweet time to make contact. I know what I'm doing."

She moved the thermal camera in slow, sweeping motions, the screen displaying a world of icy blues and vivid purples. The shelves lined with food items were mere silhouettes until a spot of contrasting warmth appeared on the camera's screen. It was a faint outline of a figure, warm against the cold backdrop, near the rear of the cooler where the dairy products and the forbidden box of peas lived.

With the recorder still running, Gwen activated the spirit box. The static hiss filled the cooler, a welcome change from the spooky silence.

"Mrs. Sweetwater? You know me. I came in every Thursday for the chicken salad sandwich and potato chips. It makes my mouth water to think about that today. I bet you hid the recipe somewhere."

The white noise seemed to pulse with potential. "If that's you, can you say your name?"

Amid the static, a voice seemed to cut through,

"Secret..." it murmured, and the temperature in the cooler dropped further, if such a thing were possible. Gwen's breath came out in a dense cloud, and the EMF meter sprang to life, its lights flashing wildly in sync with the voice.

Her equipment was reacting, but still there was no physical evidence a ghost was present. H.P. was fascinated by the entire process and felt slightly guilty that she didn't have to work nearly as hard to have a conversation with her grandmother.

"Gram Gram, show me a sign," Gwen prompted.

H.P. resisted the urge to feel angry that Gwen used her own nickname for her grandmother. It wasn't hers to use. Then she realized she'd never used that term in front of Gwen and a chill ran down her spine.

Gwen's breath became visible and a faint mist swirled at her feet. Her EMF meter wasn't just flickering; it was singing a symphony of beeps and lights, confirming the presence of paranormal activity. As she spoke, her thermal camera, peeking out from her over-stuffed backpack, detected a sudden drop in temperature, too.

The cooler lights flickered, a response that sent a ripple of excitement through H.P.

Gwen moved the video camera to cover the area where the thermal anomaly had occurred, the lens capturing everything despite the low light, thanks to its night vision capability.

Gwen's digital voice recorder, clipped next to her EMF meter, sprang to life, capturing an ambient whisper that wasn't hers. "Gwen," it seemed to say, amidst the static, "I know you."

Then, as clear as a bell through the spirit box, a series of numbers rattled off. "Four, eight, two, five," the electronic voice said.

"Eight...four...four...nine...two..."

As if playing in stereo, a soft whisper tickled her ear while also emitting a sound from Gwen's equipment. "Behind the apples! Look behind the apples!" H.P. resisted the urge to do it herself. She'd gone through the walk-in a thousand times looking for clues. Always a dead end.

Gwen wasted no time shining her light around the cooler until it came to rest on a giant box marked, "Alvin's Juicy Apples."

It sat on the top shelf, which was at least a foot over Gwen's diminutive body. The more she grunted, the more H.P. struggled to stay outside.

With one last burst of energy, Gwen pulled the box and all of its contents to the floor.

"Are you all—"

"Quick! Hand me my flashlight!"

Gwen's flashlight had rolled underneath the shelves on the opposite side of the cooler, a place H.P. was reluctant to explore. Walk-ins were notorious for attracting mice, spiders, snakes, whatever could figure a way in. By the disheveled looks of the cooler when she arrived, there was no doubt in her mind that something she didn't want to find had sought shelter there.

"Hurry up!" Gwen snapped.

Without another thought, H.P. kneeled down and stuck her hand under the shelf. Something wet, something cold and something... square. To the right was Gwen's flashlight. "Got it." She handed it over to Gwen and stood, dusting off her pants.

Gwen examined each apple from the box carefully before placing it back inside. When she was done, she stood. "Let's speak outside of the cooler."

They closed the door as they exited and both leaned against the counter. "What is it, Gwen? Who is the ghost? What do they want?" H.P. asked, wide-eyed and innocent. Her entire body tensed and her breath became shallow.

"I can't tell you for sure. What I do know, is that they played me. Those numbers? They were the product number on the apples."

"So it wasn't... my grandmother?"

Gwen removed Uncle Bash's letter jacket. "Probably not. She was a sweet, little, old lady, not a jokester."

"Oh! That's great!"

Gwen frowned. "It is?"

"Yes... I mean, no, as far as your research goes, but at least my grandmother isn't lingering around here." H.P.'s mind searched quickly for another topic. "How did you know my nickname for my grandmother? And why did you think it was her to start with?"

"I have a gift, H.P. These things just come to me if I let them. When I'm doing autopsies, I can't tell you how many times those poor folks spoke. It just happens naturally."

H.P. faked a yawn, one of her better fakes. "I'm sorry, Gwen. I'm just beat. Can we continue this conversation tomorrow? I'll help you carry your equipment."

"Oh, sure. No need to see me out. We'll catch up tomorrow."

H.P. waited until she heard the door close before re-entering the walk-in. Shining her phone underneath the shelving, she pulled out the square shape she'd felt earlier.

The box, slightly ajar, revealed a stack of old, faded recipe cards. *Gram Gram's recipes!* She picked one up and, in a voice mimicking a game show host, announced, "And what's behind recipe card number one? Four antacid chili; guaranteed to keep guests in the bathroom."

In all of her years working with Gram Gram, she'd never known her to make chili, nor anything that came with a dire spice warning. She turned the card over and read, "Answers lie at the foot of the tree."

As she pondered the message, the metallic shelves rattled gently, as if chuckling at her plight.

"Why did you send a hunter after me? Like I'm an animal? Land sakes, Hun Bun, I thought you loved me!"

"It wasn't my best idea to date," H.P. conceded. "But I really don't know who killed you, and the banker will be here any day, and—"

"Child, why would I leave you this responsibility if I didn't think you were capable enough to handle it?"

"Beats me, Gram! I've asked everyone, and nobody has a good answer!"

Honeypie Sweetwater's form lit up from behind, framed by a spectrum of blues and indigos.

"What's going on?"

H.P. felt a warm breath on her neck and her stomach twisted into knots.

"Gram Gram Sweetwater in ethereal form," Gwen whispered in awe.

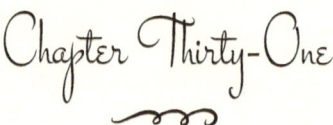

Chapter Thirty-One

"Her form is the most detailed apparition I've ever seen! I can tell she's wearing lipstick. Possibly a mauve. Could be a symbol—maybe the oppression of the American wife and mother?"

"Berried in color," H.P. and Gram Gram machine recited in unison.

Gwen still carried her voice recorder and as she brought it to her face, H.P. noticed the poor woman's hands shaking.

"...Subject wearing a red apron over a calf-length flowered dress. Even her feet, in pink sneakers, are visible. This is... incredible."

Unlike other times H.P. encountered her grandmother in the cooler, the ghost's face was kind but tinged with an undeniable sadness and urgency, yet her eyes twinkled with a mischievous glint, reminiscent of the time she'd added too much hot sauce to the taco mix.

This formal Gram Gram with makeup and all the bells and whistles also felt like a clear message: I saved the best for someone else.

Gram Gram's ghost nodded, her eyes conveying gratitude and a plea for justice. "I need you both to work together. You're so close to finding my killer. Or maybe there's more than one? I know you'll find them!"

Her gaze rested on Gwen. "Yellow isn't a good color for you, darling. Makes you look like a sick canary."

With a gust of wind that seemed orchestrated for dramatic effect, Gram Gram's ghost vanished, leaving behind a trail of cold.

Gwen and H.P. stared at each other, both with a message to share.

"You should have told me!" Gwen snapped. "Instead, you invited me here to make a fool of me. Did you and your grandmother plan this?"

H.P.'s jaw dropped. "What? No, I just didn't want to tell anyone about her until I was sure I wasn't—"

"Crazy? Yeah, I know the feeling." Gwen crossed her arms over her bright yellow sweater and leaned against a shelf. "I'll let you in on a little secret: if you make yourself indispensable to the city, they have to tolerate your crazy. Me? I'm the one who set up the emergency texts and phone calls. I can bring everyone together in a matter of minutes."

It DID sound like an admirable quality, but H.P. had absolutely nothing to offer the city. "I'm truly sorry. Gram Gram did have a reason for our visit tonight. Let me show you."

Chapter Thirty-Two

"If you was gonna start tearing the place down, you should have given me time to get my dead husband's wrecking tools out of storage."

H.P. squinted as she tried to regain her senses. She was lying on the cold tile floor of the pantry and her hands were gripping an industrial-sized bag of chocolate chips.

Now she remembered; when she told Gwen about Gram Gram's cryptic, "the answer lies at the base of the tree," message, the two of them decided to dig up what they could under the huge oak tree in front of the diner.

At two in the morning, Gwen received a message that a coroner was needed at the scene of an auto accident. H.P. promised she'd continue digging after she found sustenance and proceeded to the pantry where she must've fallen asleep. It all seemed like a dream now.

Edna and her loud coffee breath stood over H.P. The longer H.P. allowed her presence, the higher the chance that food fell into her face.

"What time is it, Edna?"

"Nearly seven. I walked around, stepped over and reached behind you for as long as I could. Now I need to get the pancake mix. Do you mind?"

H.P. pushed herself up to a sitting position. Immediately, her neck began to spasm. "Ow!" she moaned, grabbing the afflicted area.

"Let me handle that." Edna dropped two kitchen towels and kneeled on them, roughly shoving H.P.'s hand out of the way before kneading her shoulders like a double batch of sourdough bread.

"Mmm. That's amazing, Edna. When did you learn how to massage?"

"The winter your grandmother shut down the diner. I had to find something to keep my cats eating in luxury."

H.P turned abruptly. "When was that? I don't remember."

"That's because she didn't want you to know." Edna forced her back into position and continued. "There was a logging accident in the mountains outside of town. Shut down the highway for near six months. Lots of businesses went under. Your grandmother fed folks for free as long as she could. Then the money and the food ran out and she had no other option but to close."

"What did she do to survive? Did Uncle Bash

support her?"

"Not likely." Edna guffawed. "She took in sewing and did some babysitting."

Edna paused and H.P. hoped she wasn't finished. She wiggled her shoulders expectantly before Edna continued. Gram Gram's passion extended beyond the culinary arts.

As H.P. sat there with Edna's hands providing relief, the tale of the diner's temporary closure unraveled.

"Besides trying to survive, she decided to use the time to do things she'd never had time for. She took up ballroom dancing—"

"What? Gram Gram was... a dancer? Was there no end to her talents?"

Edna bent down and yelled into her ear. "If you'd hush up, I'd tell you!"

"Sorry. Please continue."

"She loved to dance. That was on Tuesdays. On Wednesdays, she volunteered down at the Chewseum. Honeypie loved telling folks about her recipes and their history." Edna clucked her tongue. "That woman had the patience of a saint."

"Sounds just like Gram Gram. She had such a passion for the kitchen, it didn't matter how many times I burned things, she encouraged me to keep going."

"Hmph. You're lucky she had the willingness to teach you."

Edna paused and H.P. wondered if she were lost in

her own memories. Someday she would ask Edna about her past, when they weren't smack-dab in the middle of a murder investigation.

"Most of all," Edna continued, "she loved to paint. They tore down the old Burrito Bucks outside of town and gave away the tiles that were on the walls. Honeypie took them home by the wheelbarrow load. When she'd finished, she donated her work to the Chewseum. You should go look sometime, instead of gallivanting all over town."

H.P. glanced down quickly with a sick feeling in her stomach. In front of her were remnants of a potato chip bag and a half-eaten apple. When did she become binge-eater?

"She always planned to take up painting again, once life settled down. But it never did."

H.P.'s mind raced as Edna spoke. At no time in their daily conversations had Gram Gram mentioned this passion. She talked about her diner, a grandchild who'd graduated from another "La-tee-da fancy school," as Gram said, and funny old movies she'd watched. Usually, H.P. fell asleep at some point during this conversation, a mistake Gram Gram would tease her about the next day.

"She loved painting that oak tree out front. Said it had just as many stories to tell as she did. The old lady is gonna take some TLC to recover from your night of destruction."

H.P. glanced around her body. Amidst the carnage was a thick layer of dirt, leaves and twigs. "What have I done?" she cried as she made a futile attempt to gather them all in her arms.

"Asked myself the same question this morning when I came in and found you passed out."

Edna placed one hand on her knee and grunted as she stood. "Go see Phil Popwell. He'll fix you right up. Best chiropractor on the coast. Tell him Edna sent ya."

Was this another one of Edna's conquests? She didn't dare ask. "I'll make an appointment, thanks. Now, what should I do about this mess?"

"Beats me. Maybe ask yourself why you spent the night here on the floor instead of home with your boy. That's where I'd start."

Edna stepped over H.P., her dress making a swishing sound as it slapped H.P. in the face. As she exited the pantry, she dropped the pancake mix to waist level, an act that allowed the heavy bag to thwack H.P. in the head.

"Oh, one more thing before I help Basil and try to take care of the morning rush, BOTH all by myself," Edna took a big gulp of air as H.P. braced for another verbal flogging. "The crunched up leaves and branches are easy enough to remove, but the soil mess is another story. Gonna need a wet vacuum and the only place I know that has them in town is the law office."

"The... law office?"

Edna nodded. "In small towns we have to double up on our businesses. Like the dry cleaners that's also a morgue? You probably forgot, what with your fancy big city condo and all."

H.P. nodded. Her brain was even more muddled than when she woke up on the floor.

"One of the partners at Fulla, Bunce and Vinegar decided to start a large appliance rental in the basement. If you go around back of the building, you'll see the sign."

Once H.P. was alone, she mulled over Edna's words. Gram Gram painted these tiles with purpose. In her pocket, she felt the recipe card she'd found the night before. She took it out and read it out loud:

"Four antacid chili; guaranteed to keep guests in the bathroom."

How odd. Why would Gram Gram even keep that in the diner?

She turned the card over and continued reading: the secret lies at the base of the tree.

As H.P. pondered the meaning of the message, a sudden cold spot enveloped her, and the metallic shelves began to rattle gently.

For some reason, she felt bitterness towards her grandmother.

"Gram Gram, in all of our talks, you've never once mentioned your hobby. You talked about ordering meat and gossiping with the soft drink supplier, but never things you liked to do. Why?"

As H.P. contemplated her next move, she couldn't shake off the feeling that someone, or something, was watching her, guiding her steps deeper into the mystery of Gram Gram's untimely death. But what was she missing?

Chapter Thirty-Three

"Don't mean to scare you, H.P."

She whipped around fast. Add paranoia to her growing list of problems. "Abe! You're a sight for sore eyes!" H.P. made a fruitless attempt to smooth her hair. She watched helplessly as bits of soil fell from her head.

If there were ever a wrong time for him to show up, it was today. She hadn't showered, hadn't even brushed her teeth, and she was fairly certain she had dust covering yesterday's clothing.

After sleeping on the floor of the pantry, there was no hope of looking presentable.

He was wearing a grey suit and jade shirt and he smelled wonderful. Like every handsome man she'd ever served in the restaurant before.

"What brings you down to the equipment rental? Don't you need to be in court or somewhere equally serious?"

Abe tossed his head back and laughed. "Not today.

The serious court dates are only held on Thursdays."

Now she just felt silly and her cheeks burned with embarrassment.

"Is there somewhere quiet we can go to talk?"

"I really need to rent a wet vacuum. I made a big mess of... What's wrong, Abe?"

His face displayed a sober mix of pity and sorrow.

"I... don't know how to tell you this, H.P., but I think you may have been right about Lem."

H.P. sank down on the office chair in Skeezy Rentals, listening as it made a whoosh sound. "Why?"

Abe closed the door behind him and wrapped his knuckles on the desk. "Yesterday, I was finishing up some paperwork for a client. I was the last one in the office. At least, that's what I thought. Tildie was spending the night at the next-door-neighbor's place, so I didn't have to worry about getting home to her. I went into the break room to make myself some coffee to help me pull an all-nighter. That's when I heard him."

H.P. felt a tingle go down her spine. This time, it had absolutely nothing to do with Abe's handsome appearance. "What was he doing? Does he have another girlfriend? Was it his wife? I knew I couldn't trust him!"

"Neither. He was on the phone with someone talking about your grandmother's will. He said he'd re-written it for her a month before she died."

"Oh."

"You sound disappointed? I thought it would

make you angry."

"That's not a reason to distrust Lem, though. You must've heard something juicier!"

Abe rubbed his strong chin with one hand and placed the other on his trim hip. "Very perceptive, Miss Sweetwater. Something made me pause in the hallway and listen to his conversation. He was telling your Uncle Sebastian that he would be happy to help him contest the will."

Anger welled up inside her. She'd welcomed Uncle Bash into their home—well, his home too, with open arms. Now it turns out he was just here to find a way to kick her and Bash to the curb?

"What else did you hear?"

"That they were going to meet today, at the coffee shop where you and I first met. He wanted to bring a friend along, but Lem told him it was better if it were just the two of them."

"What time? I've got to confront my uncle. He's been lying to me this entire time!"

"Hold on! You can't just show up, H.P., he'll figure out that I overheard his call! I was the only other one in the building last night."

The diner was filling up with regulars as she set the vacuum in the pantry and turned to leave.

"Where do you think you're going?" Edna asked accusingly. "You still haven't showered and your scent came through the door ten minutes before you did!"

"I'll be back in an hour! I promise!"

She didn't wait for Edna's sarcastic rebuttal. There

would be time for that later. Abe was waiting for her outside the diner, and together they walked over to the Jittery Bean coffee shop. All the way, H.P. tried to compose herself. If not physically, she could at least stay calm while she confronted her uncle.

They found Lem and Uncle Bash huddled together in the corner, whispering to each other as though they'd discovered the biggest secret in Misty Cove.

"H.P., let's get our stories—"

She had no time to make a plan of action with Abe. Stomping with every step, she slammed her free hand down on the table, causing everyone in the room to stop what they were doing.

Both men looked up, startled.

"You're going to clean up the mess you left today, Lem. I don't take care of blood, no matter how much you pay me!"

"What? I have no idea what you're talking about, Miss Sweetwater!"

Lem's voice was cool and collected, as though he were announcing the next song on a smooth jazz radio station.

She cleared her throat before ratcheting up her voice. "I said... I'm not cleaning up all of that blood and what was it? Brain matter? I can read the text you sent me, Lemon! I'm kind of surprised that a man who works as an attorney wouldn't have his own cleaning detail."

Uncle Bash stood and took her firmly by the

elbow.

"We're going outside," he said without emotion.

When they'd left the coffee shop and patrons could only glare at them through the plate-glass window, Bash yelled, "What in the world was that, Honey Bunny? If I didn't know better, I'd say you were accusing me of underhanded dealings!"

"Don't you Honey Bunny me, Sebastian Sweetwater! I know all about your plan to overturn the will. You want to toss me and Dex out on our ears so that you and Lem can run the diner the way you want. I wouldn't be surprised if Maddysin wasn't in on it too. I left my home and my job to come up here—"

"You don't have a home or a job, H.P. I know your whole story; how you lost everything and Mom bailed you out again and again."

He wrapped his knuckles on the brick storefront. "But that's not something I can fault you for. Heck, I've lost good jobs more 'n' I can count."

Bash adjusted the brim of his stained Misty Mountaineers cap nervously. "It's the fact that Mom bought that condo for you and you didn't have the sense to hold onto it. She believed in you, kid, and you threw it out the window."

Tears welled up in her eyes. She'd never felt this level of betrayal. Not even when Eliot left her for another woman. Uncle Bash was her protector when the other kids picked on her. He'd pull her to the side, give her a hard candy and tell her a story while the other kids rough-housed.

"You... don't know ANYTHING about my life. I've worked two and three jobs at a time, just to keep food in our mouths. Months would go by when I would only see Dex in passing, and he even started calling one of his babysitters, 'Mom.' How dare you assume I've thrown my life away. Gram Gram was proud of me 'til the bitter end. She told me every day."

H.P. hated the tears that flowed down her cheeks in a flood of emotion. Now she'd given him the upper hand. It would be much easier to turn her attention to someone equally deserving of her wrath.

"And... even... worse..." she blubbered, "Gram Gram's boyfriend was in on it with you. She trusted the both of you!"

His lack of response told her all she needed to know. She marched back inside the Jittery Bean, where customers stared at her with uncertainty. Abe was now seated at the table with Lem and the expressions they wore told H.P. something was up.

"You and Bash were conspiring to sell the diner all along. There was never any love involved. My poor grandmother went to her grave thinking you were a decent man, but all along... Did I get that right?"

The two men stared at each other, refusing to meet her gaze.

"Somebody'd better start talking, or I'll throw a fit. A big one," she warned, glaring back at those who glared at her.

"I loved your grandmother," Lem replied quietly. "She was my soulmate. But I've told you over and over.

The truth doesn't require explanation and I'm done, Ms. Sweetwater."

"HA!"

The diners turned to H.P. with stern looks on their faces. Soon, a young girl with a nametag that read, "Hi! I'm your Level Six Barista, Amber!" appeared beside H.P.

"Ma'am, you're disrupting our customers' moment of caffeinated zen. I'm afraid I need you to leave."

Amber had a squeaky voice that belied her Level Six status.

"In a minute," H.P. replied dismissively.

Amber poked H.P. on the shoulder with sharp nails for someone who worked the espresso machine all day. "Ma'am, I will be forced to call the police if you don't leave now."

Lem stood quickly and placed a hand on H.P.'s arm. "It's all right, Amber. We'll all be leaving soon."

Amber transferred her weight back and forth, from one leg to the other, waiting for a response.

"It's fine. I'm leaving."

H.P. tromped out of the coffee shop amidst claps and cheers. Nothing like making an exit, she mused.

Once she'd reached the sidewalk, she was disappointed to find Bash had disappeared.

"Miss Sweetwater, though it violates the privacy between client and attorney—"

"There's no privacy. Client is dead," she snapped.

"That's not exactly true. I drafted your grandmother's will because she asked me to help her, but it was another partner who filed it and made changes. You may be surprised to learn that you were always the recipient of the diner and her home. She never wavered in her support of you."

Those words stung like salt on a paper cut.

"Then why are you meeting with Uncle Bash? It doesn't seem ethical to me."

"Ethical in a small-town means doing your best with the resources you have. My partner, Whitaker Fulla, has agreed to represent your mother's estate. Your uncle, Sebastian Sweetwater hired him."

Lem's face never moved. It was almost as if he were a plastic doll, devoid of emotion. "Mr. Sweetwater has his own business plans. You can understand why he'd be upset that your grandmother wasn't supportive in her will. Sebastian said he also wanted to share it with your other cousins. You can see why they might be a little upset."

H.P. thought about it. None of them had contacted her since the funeral, when she was sure they would have been upset. Had they been conspiring with Bash? Was that the reason for their group's silence?

"Your uncle wants what's best for the entire family. We're going to court next week to amend the will. You're welcome to hire your own counsel."

Fat chance, she thought. Unless it was someone who worked for pancakes.

"I'll see you in court, then, Mr. Thornwood!"

H.P. pivoted away from Lem, doing her best to make him feel the way she did: insignificant.

As she was cleaning his mess, she found a crumpled piece of homework. Dex was supposed to use tools to turn some wood and nails into a creation. He was to bring both the tools and the creation and give a speech on them today.

Pulling the covers back, she found his notebook with a full page of notes about his "friend finder."

Just connect the blue tooth, press the button for the friend you're trying to find, and within seconds, you'll know right where they are.

Her heart broke into whatever pieces remained. The poor kid was bereft, unable to contact his buddies from P.S. 418 and stuck with a lying uncle and a distant mother.

Well, that was all about to change.

H.P. took the notebook and slipped on her shoes before heading out to the shed in search of the tools mentioned.

As she flipped on the light, she heard something moving around. Probably a squirrel or her fertile imagination, the same one that dreamed up the smell of Gram Gram's cookies in the shower!

Summoning all her courage, she moved the cobweb-covered bicycle tires, rusted buckets and oily rags until she found a hammer. Once more, she heard movement.

"Okay, Mr. Squirrel, I'm not playing this game. There's no point in hiding anymore. Come out slowly with your arms up and I promise you won't become roadkill."

She giggled to herself, thinking about the story she would tell her son over dinner. They would both get a kick out of it, wouldn't they?

This time, the noise she heard was definitely not a squirrel, it was a human, probably a man, clearing his throat. H.P. panicked and opened the dusty drawer next to her, pulling out the first thing she found and holding it with both hands.

"I'm giving you until the count of ten. If you enjoy your body without nail holes, I'd suggest you—"

"H.P., don't shoot! It's just me!"

From behind a rusty sprinkler head and a garden rake, a familiar face appeared.

"Eliot!" She dropped the nail gun on the ground, both relieved and upset at the same time. "What in the name of deadbeat dads are YOU doing here? Your wife is worried sick!"

The scent of his wet hair, which had smelled of baking cookies throughout their entire marriage, lingered in the air.

"I'm sorry to scare you. Sebastian said I could stay here until I got things figured out. He and Dex promised they wouldn't—"

"Wait, you involved MY son in this sick game? Eliot Jenkins, how could you? I want you out of here this instant!"

"I'll go, I promise. Just let me explain first."

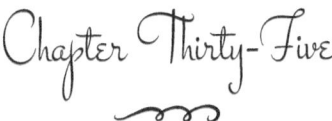

Chapter Thirty-Five

"She kicked me out two months ago. I've been working odd jobs across the country, trying to figure out exactly who I am."

"A deadbeat dad? A guy who runs off and leaves his family? Am I getting warm? Juliette never mentioned a word about kicking you out."

Eliot gave her his "shame on you!" look, which fed her anger even more. "Juliette is a proud woman who doesn't want pity, H.P. she's not like..."

Her cheeks burned as she thought about the implications of what he hadn't said. "You said you wanted to tell me something. Now's your opportunity, El."

Eliot scratched the back of his neck and stared at her feet. "Yeah, right. So... like I said, I was traveling around, working odd jobs when a guy offered me a job in Seattle, unloading freight from ships. It was good pay, and I'd never been there before, so I agreed to try it out."

She bit her tongue so hard, it was very possibly cut in two. Eliot didn't worry about his son until he ran out of money. Asking for the return of the money he left on his "visit" was going to be the next thing out of his mouth.

"It was a great gig, and I loved Seattle. The people have a different feel than the east coast; more laid back. I'd forgotten that in all my years away."

H.P. sighed. "Get on with it. I've got things to do today. Important things."

Like taking a nap, figuring out where we run next, thinking of a way to destroy Bash and the rest of this twisted family...

"When Dexter and I went for dinner, I told him everything. He convinced me that you would be supportive, and you would welcome my move back to the Pacific Northwest. That's why I came in that day to speak with you. But we know how that went."

"Oh, no, you don't, Eliot Jenkins. You're not going to turn me into the villain in this story. You said you wanted to contribute to your son's welfare, remember?"

"About that, um... later, of course." Eliot couldn't have made himself look any more guilty if he had handed her the cash from a bank robbery. "It's hard for a guy my age to find work, but Dexter came to my rescue."

"Of course he did! You're his FATHER. And now you've placed your fifty pounds of garbage on a teen boy's shoulders. You should feel ashamed, El. Very ashamed."

"He's a lot more mature than you give him credit for. Please don't judge me for what I'm about to say." Eliot paused while he attempted to reach H.P. When he did, she stepped just out of his reach.

"I've made a lot of mistakes and for that, I'm truly sorry." Eliot's eyebrows rose expectantly, as though he thought she would disagree.

"I... I was involved in the transportation of illegal prescription drugs without knowing it. The guy I met at the dock hired me to unload partyware from China. Only it wasn't partyware at all, at least, not the kind I thought. I knew I had to get out of there quickly and Dexter told me you'd moved back to Misty Cove. When we met, he gave me your Uncle Sebastian's number. Good ol' Bash found work for me, and then the three of us came up with a plan to hide me until I figured out my next move."

"Uhm... what next move?"

"I'm going to contact the authorities, obviously. But first, I need to have video evidence. Take this note and read it later, when you're not around me. It will explain everything." He stuffed a folded paper in her hand and although she felt like dropping it, her curiosity got the best of her.

"I'm paying Dexter to put it all together for me," Eliot continued. "He's been more than willing. Such a good kid we've got there."

Now there was steam coming from the top of her

head, she was sure. If possible, this day was even worse than the day she'd left her condo. The world seemed to be closing in around her.

The sound of crunching leaves on the lawn that Dex never got around to mowing alerted them to another person in the yard.

"Don't tell them I'm here!" Eliot hissed before disappearing behind the unused lawnmower.

"Thanks so much, Eliot, for dragging us into your mess and then leaving me to pick up the pieces. So typical."

She slammed shut the door of the shed and turned around, ready to face Eliot's mobster or something worse.

"You've been difficult to track down, Ms. Sweetwater!"

"Sistine, here to take control of the diner! Perfect timing—I just asked myself if things could get any worse and you showed up, right on cue."

Chapter Thirty-Six

"My uncle is planning a coup for next week, so you'll be in for a fight when it comes to the family diner. And beyond that, Honeypie Sweetwater is worth even less than she was the last time we met. Nada. Nothing."

H.P. glanced around the backyard where she and her friends used to camp in the summer months, telling scary stories after they raided Gram Gram's cupboard. The wooden fence, once painted white, was now a lackluster grey, holding a few remnants of its once cheery color. Could she scale it without collapsing in an embarrassing combination of old wood slivers and muscle strain?

"Oh, for what it's worth, my ex-husband is hiding in the shed from the cartel, or mafia, or whatever you'd call it. Maybe you can turn him over to the cops and make a few bucks." She giggled, the humor of the situation not lost on her. "I've always dreamt of Eliot paying his debt to his son with a pound of flesh."

Sistine Chapel, banker and expert tracker, appeared dumbfounded. Either disgust, fear, joy or a combination of all the above streaked across her face like bolts of lightning.

"We have several things we need to discuss. I'd like to use your restroom first, though. I stopped at a coffee shop to use theirs, but they'd just had quite the excitement, as a mentally ill woman carrying a vacuum assaulted some of their customers."

H.P. let out a long howl. She'd done nothing like that before, and boy, did it feel good. Sistine, on the other hand, was now a shade of white that didn't even look human.

"First door on the left. Watch out for my son's clothes. They tend to creep out of his bedroom."

"Don't run off this time, Ms. Sweetwater. I didn't appreciate your quick exit. We have things to discuss!"

"I promise!"

H.P. had absolutely no intention of keeping that promise. If, for no other reason than to deliver the homework Dex needed. Her fingers worked the crumpled paper in her pocket as she scurried down the street and then slowed to a comfortable pace. She was crying now, and it didn't seem right to make it appear that she was in danger.

H.P. stopped to admire the little shops along her route. Some were brand new and others looked just the same as they had decades ago when she'd gotten on her bike to visit them.

There was one place, however, that she had never

gone, even though it was in operation during her childhood.

The large, orange sign always turned her off as a kid, but even more cheesy, the Chewseum's exterior resembled a giant picnic basket, complete with woven-texture walls and oversized utensils as decorative elements.

Her feet moved forward, through the open picnic basket lid even as her brain ordered her to continue down the street.

Kids at school used to call it the Moldseum, but no one ever explained why.

She pulled on the fork and knife in the shape of an "X" and nothing happened. She yanked harder this time. "Of course! It's the expected whipped cream on my poo pie."

As she was turning to leave, the door opened and a tiny woman with tight grey curls and square, wire-rimmed glasses appeared. "Come on in, Miss Sweetwater. I've been expecting you!"

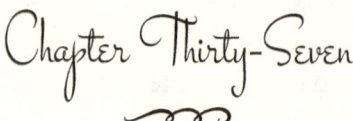

Chapter Thirty-Seven

The diminutive caretaker stood, holding the heavy door open as though she had all the time in the world. And her big smile was the nicest thing H.P. had seen all day.

"Have we met before? You don't seem familiar to me."

"We haven't, face to face, anyhoo. Etta Snackworth. I knew your grandmother pretty well, and she spoke very highly of you. She said you were a world-class chef in California."

"Gram Gram tended to exaggerate."

H.P. stepped inside and her senses were immediately encompassed like a warm blanket. "What is that wonderful smell?"

"Sourdough bread. The same starter I've used for over fifty years. Let me show you around while it's cooling."

Was this a dream?

None of this seemed real. Underneath her feet was a floor resembling a giant checkerboard picnic blanket. Overhead, an assortment of hanging lanterns shaped like fruits and vegetables lit her way.

"This is our main exhibit area."

Etta gestured widely, using bent knees to thrust her small arms as far as they would go. It reminded H.P. of the high school production of "Hoop Skirts and Muskets, the Musical," a production where she was told to deliver her six lines by gesturing so widely, the audience could see them in the next county. It was unfortunate that she missed all but the first performance, due to illness.

H.P.'s eyes moved from floor to ceiling as Etta turned and smiled. "You're appreciating our color scheme. It's not by accident, dear. Apple red, citrus orange, and berry blue dominate, while the floors are a rich chocolate brown. That's after you leave the welcome picnic cloth area."

She had completely misjudged this place, and now she understood what it meant to her Gram Gram. It was home.

"Each corridor leads to a different themed exhibit," Etta continued, oblivious to H.P.'s trip down memory lane. "Follow me, dear."

It was a lovely place, H.P. had to admit.

"In the middle of our main gallery, we have our Interactive Center, where visitors can engage in food-related activities and games. Currently, we're featuring displays explaining taste buds, flavor chemistry, and sensory experiences. A highlight is the "Taste Lab" where visitors can sample unusual flavors, including spices from all over the world."

As fascinating as this tour had been, something was pulling her into another room. "Do you mind if I browse a bit? I've had a rough day, and I need to clear my head."

"Of course! I'll be at the picnic table in the Welcome Area if you need me."

"Thanks, Etta!"

H.P. watched her leave before following her senses. She walked past the "What's Bakin', Bacon?" exhibit and turned left, where a glass door led to a dark room.

Go inside.

What did she have to lose? She turned the handle and walked inside, cringing as the door squeaked open. "Hello? Is anyone here?" she whispered, afraid of the answer.

H.P. found a light switch on the wall and flipped the lights on. In a colorful rainbow of letters, she read, "Whisk Yourself Through the History of Pies."

And underneath in smaller letters, "Exhibit funded entirely by Honeypie Sweetwater."

H.P. felt a lump in her throat. Gram Gram never mentioned a word. She walked around the large room in wonder, more impressed with each exhibit than the last.

Origins of the Pie: An exploration of the early history of pies, starting from the ancient Egyptians and Greeks, complete with replicas of these pies.

Pie in Literature and Art: Highlighted references to pies in classic literature and art, including humorous interpretations of famous pie scenes.

Around the World in 80 Pies: A vibrant section displaying pies from around the globe, with a large, interactive map where visitors could press buttons to learn about different regional pie varieties.

Pie in Popular Culture: A fun look at pies in movies, television, and cartoons, including famous pie-throwing scenes and pie-eating contests.

And in the center, The Great Pie Kitchen: A mock-up kitchen for live pie-making demonstrations and baking classes. Realizing she was exhausted, H.P. sat down on a bench shaped like a pie, with crust as the back rest and seat and blueberry filling in the middle.

With the few moments or hours she had left, maybe she could look at the evidence and figure out who killed Gram Gram. Didn't she owe her grandmother the courtesy of a name, even if it were wrong? Couldn't she give her grandmother the remaining piece of the puzzle she needed to enjoy her afterlife?

H.P. pulled out her phone and began to type:

Suspect Number One: Maddysin was broke, so there was no way she killed Gram Gram despite the air freshener found in Gram's system. It wouldn't have benefited Maddysin.

Suspect Number Two: Lem was going to cash in whether she was dead or not, it seemed. He was still a wild card.

Suspect (?) Number Three: *What about Bash?* He

253

was certainly profiting from her death. H.P. imagined him chuckling with his drinking buddies, telling them he would buy a round for the bar after he won his lawsuit.

"Oh, and I almost forgot about poor, little Cherrie," H.P. sighed. "She couldn't plan a murder if her pies depended on it."

Closing her eyes, H.P. couldn't picture any of these people in a violent struggle with Gram Gram. She was no closer to finding a murderer than when she pulled into town.

"Never give up, Hun Bun!"

She whipped around. No one else was in the room. "Etta? Do you want to join me? I could use some—"

"I'm up here, darling!" Gram Gram, in all her ethereal glory, swayed back and forth at ceiling height. A soft, purple filtered light surrounded her, and she was wearing makeup, as she only did when she went to church or Wednesday Night Bingo.

"You brought me here, didn't you?"

Gram Gram nodded, her ethereal image shimmering in the light. "Things aren't the way you see them, dear."

"Well, the way I see them right now, I've created a colossal mess!" H.P. retorted.

"No, my darling—"

H.P. held up her hand. "Hear me out, please. My son hates me for missing his presentation. Eliot brought a nightmare to my doorstep and has now involved my family. My uncle has no faith in my ability to run the diner," she paused to take a breath. "And I'm no closer to solving your murder. I'm sorry, Gram Gram. You put your faith in the wrong grandchild this time."

Gram Gram swooshed down beside H.P., bringing a warmth with her. "Oh, I don't think so. I remember how the other kids would plan social events over the weekend and then wait until the night before to tell me they couldn't work. Not you. Every single time you were scheduled, you came to work."

"That's because I had no life. I would have acted just like them if I'd had friends."

"You don't believe that. Cooking has always been your passion. That's one of the reasons why I left the diner to you. Good things are right around the corner, Hun Bun. I know that for sure." Her heart, or the spot where her heart would have been if she were still living, glowed with a shimmering yellow light. It was impossible not to stare at her and the shadow she cast.

One positive thing that had come out of all of this was that Gram Gram made death seem almost... lovely.

"This may be our last visit, unfortunately. Dex and I need to hightail it out of Misty Cove before the bank, Eliot's mob friends, or heck, maybe they work together, find us."

"Before you solve my murder? But you're so close! If you need help, reach out. In life, in death, partners are always needed."

H.P. thought quickly. If nothing else, she was

capable of giving her grandmother the last piece of the puzzle, so that she could enjoy a peaceful afterlife.

"Thanks for reminding me! I think I know who killed you, Gram Gram."

In that instant, the room felt empty. She was gone.

"I was going to tell you who killed you, but I guess you aren't interested!"

What was the word for beyond defeated. *Annihilated? Thrashed? Trounced?*

They would stop at Tildie's place on the way out of town. Dex would have a chance to say goodbye, and... shoot. What about Cinnie? Tildie looked like the kind of kid who would remember to feed a cat every day. H.P. would ask Abe while the kids talked.

Who was she kidding?

It was time to return home and face the music. Sign the papers so that the bank could deal with Bash. Maybe Dex didn't have to go to Canada with her; she would agree to let Dex live with Eliot, provided the two of them were on the next flight to Florida and worked things out with Juliette.

And what did her future hold?

Well, that was a wild card. No high-end restaurant would hire her, at least not one concerned with their reputation. The first reference check they did with a prior employer would have her application torn up quicker than butter melts on the first pancake.

Maybe there was a truck stop in a remote area of Canada that would hire her?

As she was leaving Gram Gram's exhibit, she

paused to turn out the lights. One more glance around the room wouldn't hurt. Honeypie Sweetwater had an admirable dedication to what she loved most: her family and her recipes.

Above the light switch, a large tree was painted on the wall. On its branches were photos of families who'd contributed to the Chewseum. Painted in green paint were the words, "Thank you, local families, for your donations. The Chewseum wouldn't be here without you."

H.P. rumpled the papers in her pocket as she studied the photos. Maddysin's family, her two pained sisters and equally irritated parents occupied the largest photo. There were other names she recognized as long-time residents of the community; Edna with her four dour-faced children, the owner of a local bar, and—"

"No freakin' way!"

H.P. pulled out her phone and touched the numbers quickly. "Gwen? I need your help."

Chapter Thirty-Eight

"This is a horrid way to throw a party."

Maddysin Noseinair flipped her hair behind her shoulders and swiveled around on the stool, completely ignoring the complimentary soda H.P. provided.

"It's not a party, Mad. It's a gathering of suspects." H.P. wiped the dribble of sweat that ran down her glass and onto the clean counter. Gwen agreed to close the dry cleaners so the two of them could talk through all of the evidence. The identity of the killer came to them both at the same time.

The bell over the door jingled, announcing the arrival of the last person she'd texted. Well, Gwen texted. Gwen sent out an emergency alert to all the people on H.P.'s list, telling them to gather at the Honeypie Diner for further instructions.

"I have access to all the emergency communication in the city, H.P."

Now as Gwen stood as a miniature sentinel at the door. H.P. nodded and Gwen locked them in.

Cherrie Crumbleton seemed flustered and looked totally out of her element, away from her perfectly designed pie shop.

"What in the name of trashed tiles is going on?" Edna snapped. "You tore out of here this morning like your cake was burning and then you didn't show up 'til it's dark? That's no way to run a business!"

"Can everyone hear me?"

The din of a noisy diner swallowed her small voice, so she found two tin shake makers and clanged them together until every set of unhappy ears in the room sat at attention. "CAN EVERYONE HEAR ME??"

She glanced at all the faces: Bash, Maddysin, Edna, Lem, Abe (who wasn't invited but not uninvited) Cherrie and Basil.

"Please, be patient because you'll all have your moment to shine."

"Oh, I get it now!" Maddysin's face creased, exposing layers of makeup. "This is one of those escape rooms, isn't it? My business-focused brain doesn't do well in game situations. I'll just sit here and watch."

H.P. ignored her nemesis, for now. "You all had a reason to want my grandmother dead because every single one of you wanted her Honey Pie recipe, so don't try to deny it! Mad, you needed a star dish for your new diner; Bash needed it for a diner, too, but we'll get to that in a few minutes. Eliot? You wanted to trade the recipe to the mob in exchange for your freedom." H.P. rolled her eyes. "I know how to pick 'em."

"What about the others?" Maddysin whined. "You said everyone had a reason."

"Do you remember our high school musical, 'Hoops and Hollars?'"

"What does that have to do with... of course. I played the lead role of Lillian Leavenworth, the shy but crafty mayor."

"No, Lillian Leavenworth was a madam, but let's set that aside. I practiced my part for weeks. Those four lines Evelyn Everwood delivered in the pivotal scene were all I had in the world."

H.P. fought back tears. *Not now.* "You and your friends tripped me after school, sending me flying into the metal garbage can. My nose was broken and I had to have six stitches below my eye."

She pointed to a faint scar and then scowled at the culprit. "For that reason, I'm going to be the star of THIS show. Evelyn is getting a second chance!"

The room took on the hushed silence, whether because they were afraid of what might come out of her mouth, or afraid of the character saying it wasn't clear.

"My dear, dear uncle Bash," H.P. began in a thick, Southern drawl.

Bash raised one brow as if it hadn't occurred to him that the spotlight would fall on him.

"As a child, I remember how much we kids looked forward to your arrival. You always showed up with a gift for each kid. But you always cut your visit short, because you and Gram Gram argued."

Bash shrugged his shoulders before turning back to his pie, his eyes never meeting H.P.'s.

"It hit me the other day that you and Gram argued over... well... everything. That's why it caught me off guard when I heard you'd moved in, since it seemed like that was the last place you'd go."

Bash did not try to defend himself, appearing as though he was in another world.

"The other day, while I was picking up your mess," H.P. rolled her eyes emphatically. "You really need to learn how to pick up after yourself, Uncle!"

When he didn't respond, she continued. "I was trying to clear a path to your bed. I picked up your jeans and found this."

She waved a receipt in the air, mystifying her guests.

"So, your uncle likes to eat. What else ya got?" Edna snorted.

"It meant nothing until Gwen and I started putting the pieces together. I'd never heard of Sebastiano's, so out of curiosity, I made a phone call to find out where they were located. And guess what? My Uncle, Sebastian Sweetwater, owns an upscale eatery in Tellum!"

All eyes pivoted toward Bash.

"And that's not all. He's been so successful that he bought the space next door in order to open Honeypie Too. That's according to his manager."

Bash wiped his face on a napkin and turned on the stool to face everyone. "I didn't want Mom making a big deal about it. She was always so emotional, and I knew she'd act like I was competing, and I wasn't. Now, the diner, that's different."

"I'll say!" H.P. remarked, fanning herself with a napkin. "You've been desperate to get the original recipes to all of our signature dishes, including Gram Gram's honey pie. So desperate, in fact, that you made a deal with my rotten ex-husband: he could live in our shed until he helped you find the recipes. After he'd proved himself, you would give him a job in the new diner."

"Sebastian Sweetwater! What a horrid man you are! I can see why your niece thinks you're a murderer!"

Maddysin's fake outrage was the next task for H.P. "He didn't kill Gram Gram. But you, Mad, well, you had a better motive than most." H.P. strolled over to Maddysin, for once not feeling intimidated by her five-inch heels. "But let's put that on the back burner."

She could feel Maddysin's hot breath on her back as she turned away. High school was long gone and now it was time for Honeypie Chiffon Sweetwater to have the last word. "Next, we have Edna. Gram's loyal employee since the day these doors opened."

Edna's face displayed the same sour look it wore every day of her life. If she were taking a lie detector test, she'd have the person administering the test in tears.

"It's odd that my Gram didn't leave the restaurant

to her, but Edna insisted to me that she wanted to retire. I bought that story until the day I stormed into Lem Thornwood's office. Lem was my grandmother's boyfriend, for those of you who don't—"

"We know!" They replied in unison. "Get on with it, will ya?" Edna exclaimed. "Whatever nonsense is swirling around your daffy mind, spit it out now!"

"You've visited the 'dentist' more times than I can keep track of."

Lem raised a hand and stood, towering over everyone in the room. "Let's not assume things, H.P. Edna is entitled to see me for her legal needs. It's a small town and there are few options."

The room was quiet again, at least until Edna herself stood and cleared her throat. The loud, long growl sounded like a steam ship announcing its return and H.P. couldn't be sure the old woman was going to make it.

"It's perfectly fine, Mr. Thornwood. You don't have to lie for me. It's time you knew anyway, H.P. I can't believe a secret stayed in its barrel this long, anyway."

She straightened her collar, seemingly nonplussed by the length of time it was taking her to tell her story. "Your grandmother was a kind and giving person and that's why she and Mr. Thornwood got along so well."

A hint of a smile flickered across her face. "When your grandmother made her will, she provided for me and my mother to go on an Alaskan cruise. Awful nice of her."

Edna opened her mouth as though another lost ship might return, but then thought otherwise. "But Honeypie Sweetwater knew everybody's secrets, and I was no exception. The reason we stopped making your grandmother's recipes after she died was that I couldn't read them in the first place. I didn't want to make them by memory, because my mind isn't what it used to be. Honeypie knew I couldn't read, so she asked Mr. Thornwood if he'd teach me. That way, mother and me wouldn't get lost in Alaska and miss the boat."

H.P.'s cheeks burned with embarrassment. "I'm so sorry, Edna—and Lem—I misjudged you both!"

Chapter Thirty-Nine

"Can we all leave now, or are we hostages?" Maddysin snapped.

"Not yet. Patience is not one of your strong suits, Mad, but I promise, I'm almost done. I can't get to the main event before addressing Abe. I know exactly what your role was in Gram Gram's death."

Abe Bunce furrowed his brow, making H.P. feel just awful. It didn't matter though. They'd be gone soon and Abe would become a distant memory. "Whatever you're accusing me of, you're way off base. I've never done anything that would embarrass my daughter. At least nothing a few months of therapy wouldn't cure."

"Abe, Gwen and I looked online and discovered you were the executor for Gram's will, and the person who will continue the good she's done in the community, like the addition to the Chewseum. Thank you for all that you've done for her."

He nodded, his face taking on a more relaxed look.

"Now for the good stuff." H.P. rubbed her hands together with a twinkle in her eye. As soon as the room was quiet, she gestured broadly, just as she had during her one performance. "Maddysin, you've got yourself a boyfriend, you little vixen, you!"

"Whom I spend my time with is none of your business!" she retorted. "And now I'm going home to feed my dog. Puffikins has to eat her produce before six or she gets tummy trouble."

Gwen thwarted Maddysin's attempt to leave, catching her mid-flounce.

"I may be half your size, but I've taken enough self-defense classes I could put you on the ground in ten seconds, flat."

"Thanks, Gwen. You're outstanding."

"In a minute. I wouldn't care whom you dated if it weren't important to this story. The first time I thought Basil met my uncle, Bash said Basil looked familiar. When I found out about Bash's restaurant, I called the previous owner, and guess what? Basil was their star chef. That is, until he started pitting employees against one another."

H.P. smiled. She couldn't help it. "According to his former employer, and the one before that, Basil's goal was to tank the restaurant so he could buy it on the cheap. He owns a number of restaurants, some of which are failing miserably."

"They most certainly are not!"

"Hold on, Basil. There's more. Everything was

going according to Basil's plans until the owner's health declined because of his employees' constant arguments. He shut the place down with no notice. Tough break, Basil." She gestured again, this time narrowly missing Edna's face.

"Uncle Bash came into the picture as the new owner, changing the name to Sebastiani's. He interviewed you, Basil, and when he checked your references, he was told that your steaks tasted like they'd been cooked over a car engine."

"Ohh! Yeah! I remember you now. Two people said you were a toxic mess and one more said he thought you were a psychopath and didn't understand why I'd even consider hiring you!"

"Your mistake, Uncle Bash, was in telling your new staff about Basil. Word got back to him and, well, let's just say his biscuits were burned."

"Maybe when YOU cook them, but I'm a highly-trained chef," he sniffed. "My food—especially my steaks—are the finest on the west coast. I've been written up twice in Chop Talk."

"And strangely, you're still working in a diner. But that's not really because you HAVE to, is it, Basil? You were so angry that Bash didn't hire you, that he besmirched your good name, that you did some research and found out that his mother owned a restaurant too. You were going to make him pay, one way or another."

"Maddysin, it's your turn to shine, darling."

H.P. gestured toward the already-flustered

Maddysin, who was picking imaginary lint from her cashmere sweater.

"The former owner of The Snobby Lobster was kind enough to message me a photo from their last Christmas party, just to confirm we were talking about the same guy."

H.P. pulled her phone from her purse and held it up for everyone to see. "You can see Basil, seated on the left. But there's another familiar face. Can anyone—"

"That's Maddysin Noseinair, front and center!" Edna's excitement was the first true emotion she'd shown.

"Yes, it sure is. I asked the owner why she was in the photo, and he said she was the girlfriend of their head chef, Basil Thymeson."

"Oh, no!" Lem's hand flew up to his mouth.

"Just because we're dating, doesn't mean—"

"Hold on to your shorts, Mad, I'm not done. Maddysin bought herself an air freshener company, just for kicks and giggles. Her secret idea was to develop a meal-themed air deodorizer. Every hour, the scent changed to a different course. She thought it would be a great addition to her new diner, the one she would open here once she convinced Gram Gram to sell. Gwen? Care to jump in?"

Gwen stood on a booth seat, something H.P. would normally discourage, but today was an exception.

"When Mrs. Sweetwater died, she had formalde-hyde, petroleum distillates, and p-dichlorobenzene in her system, commonly used in air freshener. This was injected between her toes as she lay sleeping, so that when she tried to get up, her body wouldn't move. Instead of standing, she slumped over the side of the bed, trying desperately to reach her phone."

H.P. felt a lump in her throat. Poor Gram Gram. She didn't deserve that ending.

"After the person injecting the air freshener finished, the next killer came in, expecting to find Mrs. Sweetwater in bed. She was a fighter, however, and somehow regained enough movement to fight back."

H.P.'s eyes glistened with tears and she nodded to Gwen to continue.

"That's when Mrs. Sweetwater fell on something that was too wide to be scissor blades. Near as we can tell, she fell on a chef's knife."

"And the only person here who has nice chef knives is..."

"Basil Thymeson!" The group said in unison, as if guessing in a trivia quiz.

"Yes! Correct! But that still leaves another killer on the loose. The person who injected Gram Gram with the..."

"Formaldehyde, petroleum distillates, and p-dichlorobenzene," Gwen repeated. "Didn't mean to interrupt you, H.P." She thumped on her skull as she muttered, "Bad Gwen! Bad Gwen!"

"Thanks, Gwen. We already know that Basil had a motive to kill Gram Gram—he wanted to get back at

Uncle Bash. But Maddysin had one too. She wanted those recipes."

Maddysin opened her mouth to protest.

"No, Mad, I'm not putting the spotlight on you. Your only crime here is poor taste in boyfriends. And shoes. Those five-inch heels are ridiculous for a woman who is already almost six feet tall. All kidding aside, I looked at your calendar and discovered you had a retreat called, 'Tall and Too Pretty,' booked that weekend. Ugh."

"Let me see if I understand," Abe said. "You're telling us that Maddysin and Basil planned your grandmother's death?"

H.P. nodded enthusiastically. "Yes! No. There were two people involved, but I haven't finished."

"Well, hurry it up! Some of us aren't getting any younger!" Edna growled.

"I promise I'm almost done, Edna. I was perusing the Chewseum, a delightful place by the way, when I noticed the tree my grandmother painted. On each branch is a big donor, but at the bottom, the foundation, are two families. Maddysin's and the Thymeson family. Lovely people, with three kids—a chemist who knows a lot about air fresheners ingredients and what they do to a body, a professional chef, and..." H.P. did one more sweeping gesture, just for old times' sake. It was her moment to shine. "And the pièce de résistance."

"By process of elimination, we know Edna didn't kill her. I checked with her mother and the two of them enjoyed too many Happy Hour Slick Slugs at the Tipsy Turtle the night of February 1st and slept until noon the next day. It wasn't Lem, he genuinely loved her. There's only one person left here who hasn't been accounted for. Someone, unbeknownst to all of us, is the third sibling in Basil's family and the only girl."

Cherrie Crumbleton pulled a bright red gun from her bright red bag and pointed it directly at H.P.'s head. "Golly gosh. This was all whipping up as smooth as a homemade crème until you moved in." Cherrie's eyes sparkled and her face was creased by an evil grin. "When I found Sebastian's home town, I set up shop. Yes, there were lots of customers at Honeypie Diner, but with my flair for baking and Basil's skill as a chef, all we needed were those recipes and we'd open our own chain of diners."

She glared at Bash. "You could have avoided all of this, you know."

"What happened to my mother? What did you do?"

"My brother and I watched her house for an entire year. That woman never wavered from her schedule. Open the window at nine p.m., close it at ten a.m. Basil came in first and injected the poison, and then I waited. I was shocked when she put up a fight, knocking my gun out of my hand. Luckily, my brother was still there. He pulled one of his chef knives from his satchel, and—"

"You'll have to kill me, because I'm not giving up my grandmother's recipes," H.P. said calmly.

"This place is going under. I've been taking money from the safe every month and I know for a fact that you're down to your last few dollars!" Basil spat.

No wonder the diner books never made sense!

"Sweetiekins, I've made delicious deviants disappear for less." Cherrie cocked the gun as H.P. closed her eyes, waiting for the blast.

"That's all we need for now."

To everyone's surprise, the sheriff appeared. Gwen's disappearance had gone unnoticed until now, when she jumped from behind the sheriff to see what was happening.

Chapter Forty

The entire diner erupted in cheers.

Luckily, the sheriff brought his junior partner and also his nephew along to help with the arrests. "It would have been a real quandary if there were only one set of handcuffs and two prisoners," Gwen said, stating the obvious. "There's only been one time I had to detain a criminal for the police. When he got sassy with me, I flipped him on his back and cuffed him to the exam table. Cried like a child."

H.P. watched wistfully as the diner cleared out. It was exhilarating, knowing she and Gwen had solved her grandmother's murder.

"Hope you're not going anywhere, Ms. Sweetwater," the sheriff said on his way by with Basil. "We could use more good folks like you in Misty Cove."

H.P. smiled, unwilling to share the mess her life was in.

"Oh, I never told you about the DNA I found on Maddysin's letter opener."

"You said it was a relative of mine, right?"

Gwen glanced to one side and then the other. "A relative of BOTH of you. From my research, I discovered that you and Maddysin share a great grandfather on your father's side. I can research that if you want?"

"That's for another day, Gwen. I've had just about enough excitement today."

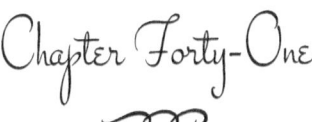

Chapter Forty-One

"That's the whole story, Gram Gram."

H.P. sat on an overturned bucket in the walk-in, where she'd spent the last hour telling her grandmother's ghost about the capture of the two people responsible for her murder.

"It still crumples my rumpus that I didn't see through Basil's shenanigans earlier. He seemed like such a nice man, always offering to help outside of work hours. Do you know, he even helped paint the living room?"

She found the dusty blue paint in the living room of H.P.'s, or rather, the bank's home, depressing. "He was casing the joint, Gram Gram. He wanted those recipes."

"Oh, that reminds me, there's still the matter of my will."

"You don't have to tell me anything. It's okay if you left the rest of your property to another grandchild.

I've been meaning to say something ever since I arrived."

H.P. couldn't look Gram Gram in the eyes while she admitted to her role as The Sweetwater Family's Colossal Failure. Instead, she stared at the forbidden peas, the ones she was never allowed to touch.

"I'm afraid I have to sign the diner and your home over to the bank in San Francisco. You know about my restaurant that failed—"

I'm so sorry, baby girl. You worked your rear end off to get that place off the ground. It's not your fault a pan-what's-a-doodle came along."

H.P. tried so hard to be stoic, but for the second time in three days, she found herself immersed in an ugly cry. "Then came a string of restaurants that fired me. At the end of the day, I knew I didn't belong. I should have gotten a job as an insurance adjuster or something."

"You wouldn't have fit there either, Hun Bun. Your place is right here, in your diner." Gram Gram's ghost shimmered above her, like a light show using blue glitter.

"I... I... this could have been a new start for Dex and me. But I blew it, just like I blow everything. The banker lady found me, and..."

It occurred to H.P. that she hadn't seen Sistine since she was surprised in the backyard. Did Eliot's mob guys find her first? Maybe Eliot's mob guys stuffed her body in the shed, behind the lawn fertilizer?

"Why on earth would you get rid of my legacy, child?"

It hurt to confess, but she thought the old woman knew what a mess her granddaughter was. "My money troubles, of course."

Gram Gram floated in a circle above her head before stopping on the large container of frozen peas. "It's time you opened this."

"The... peas?"

Gram had been so insistent that H.P. not touch them and now they were some sort of prize?

"Cool your tool. She's coming!"

The door to the walk-in squeaked as it opened slowly, revealing Edna Snarlwood.

"Edna, I was just taking inventory. I'll be out—"

"You were gonna tell her, weren't 'cha?"

H.P. cocked her head to the side and placed one hand on her hip. "Edna, whom are you talking to? There's no one here but you and me."

Edna's eyes widened as she pointed up. "And your grandmother. This is where we have all our conversations."

H.P.'s glance traveled from the ghost to the old woman and back again. "Wait, so all of this time..."

"We—me and your grandmother—planned the whole thing." Edna looked quite pleased with herself. "Your grandmother's been worried about you and she knew you needed to come home to Misty Cove. It's been our main topic of conversation for months now."

H.P.'s mouth must've been hanging open, because

Edna reached over and lifted her chin. "How are we gonna get H.P. back home to take over? What will it take?"

"I still don't understand. Why was it so important for me to come back?"

"I was ready to retire. Lem and I were going to move somewhere warm and the other grandchildren weren't diner material, I'm afraid."

"Well, why didn't you just tell me that from the beginning, and save us both the drama?"

"Edna, you take this one."

Edna nodded solemnly before pushing H.P. back down on her makeshift stool. "When Honeypie died, it just about did me in. I came over after the service and decided I'd clean out the walk-in. I was sure the diner would close without another generation of Sweetwaters here to run it. That's when she appeared like an angel. Honeypie told me who killed her, and we decided right then and there to let you figure it out for yourself."

H.P. blinked twice before massaging her temples. It was too late to wonder if she were dreaming. Too many months had gone by. "I'm still trying to wrap my head around this. Gram Gram knew all along who killed her? This is not the way to go about convincing me to stay, you know."

"We see it all on this side, kiddo. And you didn't need a lick of help from me. I always knew you were the smartest of my grands. I can now confirm that to be true. Especially your cousin, Peaches. Egad!"

H.P. swallowed hard. "There's no more money. I can't even pay Edna this month, and I doubt we'll ever recover all the money that Basil and Cherrie stole."

"Edna, we were about to get to the peas."

"Oh, right. Out of the way!" Edna commanded.

H.P. dutifully moved so that Edna could dig through to the back of the shelf. She pulled out a plastic tub that had a crack in the center of the lid.

"That needs to be thrown out, Edna. It's not sanitary."

Edna growled at her before pulling off the lid and exposing its contents. "Two million in small bills. That's what's left after I paid off your banker friend. Now, don't go thinking you're entitled to a penny more. The rest is in an account Mr. Thornwood is in charge of to give to charity."

Today had been one of the worst and best of her entire life. "I don't know what to say!"

"Edna, you forgot something!"

"Oh, right." She dug through the pile of bills and produced a money bag. Unzipping it, she revealed its contents, all the rest of Gram Gram's recipes.

"You don't have a choice now, darling," Gram Gram said happily.

"You're officially a resident of Misty Cove."

Wacky Waffle Whacker

"I grew up in a small town in Colorado, where the folks ran a diner. Nice place, as long as you weren't hankering for a fluffy omelette."

Honeypie Chiffon Sweetwater, or H.P. as she was known, glanced out the window of Honeypie Diner wishing she could join the kids whacking each other over the head with their books. Frances Flapjack was the seventh person she'd interviewed for the job of head chef and definitely the chattiest.

Blue, the guy who smoked weed during their interview, was the only one to come close to Frances in qualifications. On top of that, Edna, her grandmother's friend and the longest employee, threatened to quit if H.P. didn't hire someone today.

"Frances, let's talk salary."

H.P. studied the woman in front of her. Frances was built like a tank and wore a sleeveless tank top to their interview to show off her "guns." One of her arms boasted a colorful tattoo sleeve featuring her favorite breakfast items: pancakes, eggs, and bacon, along with baking tools like whisks, spatulas, and mixing bowls. A professed, "breakfast nut," she wore a gold necklace around her neck with a gold pancake medallion.

"Oh, you're hiring me? Just like that? I thought there'd be a second interview, with your employees and whatnot."

Frances used one finger to slide her bright red glasses frames up the bridge of her nose as she leaned forward.

"The 'whatnot' is that we are desperate for a new chef, after our last chef left unexpectedly. We need someone yesterday." H.P. felt a trickle of sweat roll down her back. It wasn't so easy being on this side of the interview table.

"I sold The Sunnyside after the folks passed, and boy I made a full stack with butter on the side. Bought myself a home-on-wheels and set off for parts unknown."

Frances smiled, giving H.P. a glimpse of the large space between her two front teeth.

"Now, I like to travel around and see this big, beautiful country," Frances continued. "All I ask by way of salary is enough to keep gas in my RV and food in the bowl for Sir Sizzleworth, my pup."

Edna Snarlwood, who was waiting on the sheriff at the opposite end of the narrow room, glanced up as if on cue. Though it shouldn't have been possible from such a distance, Edna glared at H.P. before mouthing, "do it, or I walk."

As difficult as it had been to find a new chef, replacing Edna would be twice as hard. She was the heart and soul of the diner, working there for over thirty years.

Edna came out of retirement to help H.P. and threatened daily to quit again if H.P. didn't find more help. A high school girl came in from two until close, but that wasn't enough for Edna.

H.P. half-stood and leaned over the shiny tabletop, offering her hand. "You're hired, Miss —"

"Just call me Frankie." She shook H.P.'s hand so vigorously that H.P. felt her teeth chatter. "Oh, and one more thing. I only make breakfast items. Burgers, fries and anything else, you'll have to handle burgers, fries and anything else that comes under the heading of a lunch item."

That was a plot twist H.P. didn't see coming. "Erm...would you excuse me for a moment? I need to get your paperwork." As she exited to the booth, Frankie stood as though frozen in place. "Was there something else?"

"No, ma'am. Just...thank you!" Frankie saluted her with a precision that would have made any general proud.

As soon as she'd reached the kitchen, H.P. glanced around. The temporary chef who was leaving town the next day was humming to himself. Luckily, he used ear buds after the breakfast rush, so it took Herculean efforts to get his attention. He had no idea what was about to happen.

H.P. opened the door to the walk-in cooler and stepped inside. "Gram Gram?" She hissed. "You come here this minute! I have a bone to pick with you!"

The smell of her grandmother's signature honey pie filled the cooler first, followed by an ethereal blue light. Her grandmother's spirit filled the center of the light, bringing a warmth to the otherwise cool space.

"What's wrong, Hun Bun?"

"You specifically told me to hire the next person who came through the door." H.P paced back and forth, narrowly missing a box of carrots on the floor. "Hun Bun, don't give up. The next person who asks for an application is the chef you've been waiting for."

Gram Gram's eyes widened as her figure lowered down, closer to her granddaughter. "And wasn't she? Her qualifications are stellar!"

"I've trusted you ever since I took over ownership of the diner. Every day you give me solid advice on something diner-related. But this woman is a nut. No, she's one egg short of an omelette. She just told me that she won't make any of the lunch items on the menu!"

"My darling, you can't afford to be picky. With just you, Edna and that new teen you've hired—"

"The jury's still out on CeeCee Crepe. She giggles more than she works."

"I've never let you down, have I? Frankie is the right choice."

A brisk knock on the cooler door startled them both. "Ma'am? You'd better come out here."

It had to be serious if it had gotten his attention.

"H.P. opened the door slowly. "What's the problem?"

The chef pointed to the front of the diner, where people were shouting. Rushing to the front of the house, she found Frankie straddling Principal Nunsense from the local high school. His arms were pinned behind him and he flailed about on the floor. "I'm not the enemy! Please release me, Madam!"

"Frankie! Let him go! He's a respected member of our community!" H.P. was horrified. How was she going to hire this woman now? The last thing she needed was lawsuit.

"It's all right, Ms. Sweetwater!" Principal Nunsense said in a muffled voice.

Frankie let go of his arms and stood, offering him a hand up.

"The man came in here yelling about murder. Frankie doesn't mess around with those words. I took him to the ground until he gave me the facts."

H.P. stared at them both, wide-eyed.

"You were...okay with that, Principal Nunsense?"

"Quite. I appreciate someone who puts safety first." He smoothed the front of his silver suit and glanced at Frankie with adoration. "The way you took me down was, well, it was art in motion."

The sheriff approached them with a somber look on his face. "Mr. Nunsense, I've confirmed your statement." He turned to the gathering crowd of patrons. "I need everybody to stay calm."

The guy at Table Two yelled, "how are we supposed to stay calm when there was another murder? Is Misty Cove dealing with a serial killer?"

Read here!

Acknowledgments

Thanks as always to my wonderful worldwide family. Your strength and love has given me the inspiration to do what I love. Molly Burton, you're always upbeat and ready to create, no matter how things are going in your world. Doug, your support and love gets me through the dark days.

Thank you!

About the Author

Joann Keder is a USA TODAY Bestselling author who has won numerous awards. She spent her formative years (over 40) living on the plains of Nebraska. When she and her husband chose to make a move to the Pacific Northwest, she came to an agreement with her soul that it was time to start writing.

Today, she creates stories about strong women, their quirky sidekicks and the paths they choose. When she's not writing, she and her husband enjoy nature, a good chocolate and spending time with family. Not necessarily in that order.

Also by Joann Keder

Piney Falls Mysteries

Welcome to Piney Falls

Saving Piper Moonlight

Tales of Naybor Manor

Lavender's Tangled Tree

The Twisted Stitch Society

Kinundrum

Charming Mysteries

Oceanberry Blues

Tangerine Troubles

A Lime in Time

Emory Bing Mysteries

The Case of the Half-Baked Bing

The Case of the Rootbeer Bungle

The Case of the Fudged Features

The Case of the Chunky, Funky Monkey

The Case of the Clairvoyant Carrot

The Case of the Vegan Vixen

The Case of the Cream Cheese Caper

Pepperville Stories

The Story of Keilah

Secrets and Sunflowers

Franniebell and Purple Wonder

Be the first to hear about new releases! Sign up for my newsletter here:

http://www.joannkeder.com

www.ingramcontent.com/pod-product-compliance
Lightning Source LLC
Chambersburg PA
CBHW031205020726
47499CB00002B/499